A NOVEL

TROPIC FURY

Christopher Gale

WILDSIDE PRESS

TROPIC FURY

Cover Painting by Harry Schaare

✿ One

JOE STARK was a man of many names.

It was part of his business.

Jacob Benz of Shanghai, LeRoy Adler, a Tokyo importer; Arthur Wells, a jade connoisseur traveling in Burma—those he had been and many others. But today he was himself. Officially he appeared on the rolls of the United States Navy as Joseph Edward Stark, age thirty-two, rank of lieutenant commander, together with a notation stating he was attached to the staff of Captain Milton Durling, Office of Naval Intelligence, 14th Naval District, Pearl Harbor, Hawaii.

On the second day of February, 1942, he sat hunched before a pile of documents when his phone rang briskly. He answered without removing his eyes from the papers:

"Commander Stark."

"Captain Durling would like to see you immediately, Commander." The voice of his superior's pretty Wave yeoman brought the wisp of a smile to his lips and he injected a bit of honey into his answer.

"Why sure, sweetheart."

"Thank you, Commander." Formal, all very formal, but he caught a slight inflection in her voice that told him more than words ever could. Mary Wendell, Yeoman First Class and a redhead to boot. He liked redheads. Cupping the mouthpiece he lowered his voice.

"Tonight?"

A slight pause followed before the soft answer came: "That would be grand."

"Have a seat, Joe." Captain Durling threw a fast glance at Stark and as quickly returned his attention to an official-

5

looking document he had been reading. A cigarette dangled from his lips.

"Thank you, sir," Stark murmured, idly wondering what the Old Man wanted.

He considered Durling the Navy's sharpest, if not highest-ranking spy master—if one could call him that. Gray and plump and fifty-two, he looked anything but a man whose whole adult life had been spent in the all-important but little understood command designated ONI: Office of Naval Intelligence.

Durling dropped the paper to his desk and looked up, studying him gravely before saying, "How would you like to go to Sumatra—Palembang?"

Sumatra! Wham—just like that, an island in the middle of the Japanese noose. The approach had been typical of Durling. He had the lightning thought that the Japs were poised to make a grab for the rich oil fields there. Suppressing his surprise, he asked quietly, "Lieutenant Driscoll?"

"Missing . . ." The hard, flat pronouncement gave the word an air of finality.

Exit Driscoll, Joe thought, feeling a momentary stab of remorse. Driscoll had shown promise, and Sumatra had been his first major assignment. He sighed deeply and leaned back. Admirals wrote off ships; ONI chiefs wrote off men, but neither did so without feeling. The hardness in his superior's voice in reality reflected an expression of loss. So Driscoll hadn't hacked it. The blue eyes were watching him as he answered. "Palembang sounds fine—something like a Chinese Fourth of July."

Durling grunted and as he flicked his eyes toward a large wall map of the South Pacific, his own followed. Isolated markers had already reached Rabaul and Kavieng. Australia looked like a dead pigeon. So did the whole of the South Pacific.

Durling said conversationally, "There's the problem of getting you in. The Japanese are expected to sweep over the Dutch East Indies within days. They need the oil—which they'd better not by a damned sight get," he added

6

crisply. Stark noted he didn't say anything about getting out again, nor did he ask.

Durling laid his cigarette in an ash tray and added, "Here's the problem. . . ."

Sumatra.

Behind Stark lay the long, circuitous jump by plane, surface ship and submarine. The stinking harbor built out of dredged mud and the ramshackle Dutch customhouse were fleeing to his rear. Ahead, deep in the jungles, lay Palembang, the center of a multimillion-dollar oil industry.

Clackety-clack, clackety-clack. The wheels of the ancient train rang harsh in the still, muggy air, its antiquated carriages swaying and groaning as it rounded the curves. He shifted on the hard seat to get more comfortable. Half a dozen Malays squatted on the floor around a chess board, seemingly unmindful of the jolting and noise, while a turbaned Moslem sat opposite him, eyes closed. He wore a native sarong with a dagger thrust into the waistband.

Clackety-clack, clackety-clack. The smoke from the locomotive swirled backward, stung Stark's nostrils; in the oppressive heat his standard tropic whites clung to his lank body, already drenched. He pushed back his sun helmet and wiped the sweat from his brow, thinking it was worse than Rangoon.

Rangoon. His memory stirred. He had been sent there last year to find a man who had codes to sell. Japanese military codes. His contact had been Aspara, a native girl whose name meant *Celestial Nymph*—their coming together had been quite natural.

She had a body, small and brown, little breasts like russet apples, a slender, lovely face; to him she had revealed a passion never indicated by the innocence in her eyes. He remembered the first time. She had undressed, quite naturally, standing in profile, letting her clothes drop around her feet—had turned. Straight and lovely, her lips slightly parted, she had come straight into his arms, murmuring wants into his ear. Aspara—she had denied

7

him nothing. Now Rangoon was far away. He sighed regretfully.

Dark, opaque forests flashed by on each side of the railroad tracks, growing out of brackish water—liana, palm, mangrove, fern and strange twisted trees for which he had no names. Off to one side meandered a tributary of the Musi River.

Clearings sped by where rows of women naked to the hips chanted, digging into the soil with long pointed stakes as they prepared for the next planting. Their voices came as a low dirge, rising and falling to the rhythm of the plunging spears. Behind them rose a mountain chain, appearing like the profile of some prehistoric lizard astride the earth. *Bukit Barisan,* the Parade of Mountains. The name came from some half-forgotten memory as he groped with his geography. The volcanic peaks that formed the lopsided backbone of Sumatra were part of a system that originated in Lower Burma, its peaks forming the island chain.

This was the land of the Malays—Gayos, Achinese, Bataks, Kerintjis, the fierce nomadic Kubus of the Djambi Mountains whose dark, dwarfish figures and frizzled hair revealed their Negrito forebears, and dozens more. Indians, Arabs, Chinese and Koreans were mixed in, as well as a handful of Whites—Dutch, German, English, American. The latter were the *tuans,* the masters—the gods of the earth. He smiled at the thought. The vast mass of slim brown bodies had begun to suspect that the white man was somewhat less than a god, a belief espoused and spread by the little yellow conquerors now riding a flood tide out of the Land of the Rising Sun.

Saito the Shadow. He contemplated the name, fretful because he could attach no information to it. *Saito promised freedom, death to the oppressors, was spurring the natives to rebellion. . . .* That was the sum total of his knowledge. The name was new to the ONI rolls, a faceless man paving the way for the Japanese seizure of the rich Sumatra oil fields.

Stark's job was to assure that the richest prize of all,

8

the Sumatra Independent Oil Company, was destroyed the hour the Japanese invaded. But not before. In case of a miracle and the islands held, the Allies would need the oil, every drop. In essence, he had a fifty-million-dollar decision on his hands.

Perhaps he'd be lucky. Up till now he hadn't flubbed an assignment. He'd been shot, stabbed and clubbed, but he'd always returned the goods, in the process winning Durling's unspoken approval. From Tokyo to Australia and from California to Canton, he'd seen them all, with a few dozen other places thrown in. In the meantime, he'd gone up the ladder, climbing toward his four stripes and, perhaps if he were lucky, Durling's job some day. Los Angeles, where he had spent his youth, seemed incredibly remote. *But who was Saito?*

When the toy engine roared out of the jungle and across a small plain, the grotesque caricature of a city rushed into view—Palembang. Its hundred thousand people included somewhat less than two thousand Europeans and Eurasians. Swamps, stilted homes, naked children and a great stone mosque ushered it in. The train chugged and puffed, grinding to a halt alongside a weather-beaten wooden station, and he rose from his hard seat, picking up his traveling bag.

As the stir in the car ceased, he realized the native passengers were waiting for him to leave. Tuan—he had to act like a tuan or lose face. Walking between the waiting Malays, he descended to a warped platform, glanced curiously around and strode out to the muddy street. Between the town and coast lay a gently falling, jungled plain split by the tributaries of a dozen rivers.

A wild land, he thought, ancient yet new. Rubber had brought it to life. First rubber, then oil. Now the tuans were moving in, bleeding the land of its black gold; but a restless wind was rustling among the people of the East.

He swept his eyes over the street, a sodden thoroughfare lined with barracks, flimsy Chinese hotels, churches, small shops—homes that were incredibly filthy shacks. The European businesses and residences were grouped to-

9

gether, standing like an oasis amid the ramshackle native quarters. His nostrils caught the acrid tang of gasoline. Downstream along the Plaju lay the Royal Dutch Petroleum Company, across from another foreign-owned refinery.

His own interests lay upstream, just beyond the edge of town. There, before the Musi forked, lay the giant Sumatra Independent Oil Company, which was largely American-owned and -operated. That was his target. He swung his eys around the street, spotted an ancient Ford cab and started toward it, hand raised. A slim, ageless Malay sprang out from behind the wheel, bowed respectfully and opened the rear door.

"Sumatra Independent," he ordered, as if he'd made the trip a thousand times before.

The native eyes quickly assessed him. "Yes, tuan."

❁ two

"DRISCOLL'S DEAD," Mike Hawker explained, "killed by a native."

Stark thoughtfully eyed the beefy superintendent of Sumatra Independent across the scarred desk in the latter's office, which in reality was a side room of his house. His florid face dripped sweat, and a soiled white shirt clung to his barrel-shaped chest. Dark stubble masked his face, broken by a livid scar across one cheek. He reeked of tobacco.

Hawker was his contact, just as he had been Driscoll's. Stark had covered his scant file briefly: American, age forty, native wife, twelve years on Sumatra during which he'd risen from driller to his present position. Thoroughly dependable. Nothing extraordinary in the record. He dismissed the knowledge.

"Catch the killer?" he asked.

Hawker shrugged. "No clues—didn't see it. Just found the body."

"Where?"

"On the veranda outside." He gestured toward the door.

"How did you know it was a native?"

"Blowgun," Hawker replied imperturbably. "On this island that spells Malay." A slightly contemptuous note had crept into his voice. Stark disregarded it.

"Can you assign any possible motive?"

"No, none at all, unless he stepped on someone's toes."

"Hardly a reason for murder," Stark commented wryly. "Did anyone know he was ONI?"

"No—except me, of course. I was passing him off as a wheel from the main office," Hawker explained.

"Now I'm the wheel," Stark observed absently. "Mind briefing me on his moves while he was here—who he talked with and where he went?"

Hawker did, shortly, and when he finished Stark knew very little more than before. Driscoll had been on the island several weeks, had talked with a few people and had died. Nothing more.

Stark tried a different approach. "How many white men have been killed by blowguns around here lately?"

The superintendent looked startled. "Why, no one," he finally admitted. "A Dutchman got picked off that way in town but that was a couple of years ago."

"A bit unusual, eh?"

"You might say that." Hawker smiled grimly. "Everything's unusual in this country."

"Meaning what?"

"Meaning nothing. This ain't Tulsa, that's all."

"That your home?" Stark asked politely.

Hawker grunted. "It is, or was. Damned if I know after twelve years in this hellhole." His lips formed a feeble grin. "I guess by now I've gone native."

He watched the superintendent's face and carefully asked, "Ever hear of a man named Saito?"

Hawker's eyes grew curious. "Driscoll asked that same question," he replied obliquely.

"I wouldn't be surprised. What did you tell him?"

"Nothing. The name didn't ring a bell." He smiled quizzically. "Especially that shadow part—he made the guy sound like something out of Scotland Yard."

Stark dropped the subject and asked about the fields.

"We're ready," Hawker promised bluntly. "We're planting dynamite under all the shops and heavy equipment and mining the tank areas with fire bombs. Sledge hammers and acetylene torches will take care of the rest. We plan to blast the main pipeline every couple of hundred yards."

"Will you have time?"

"Sure." Hawker's voice was confident. "Those damned Japs won't get up the Musi that quick. Not with the Dutch and English planted downstream. We're at the end of the line, so to speak."

"Could you blow the works today if you had to?"

Hawker looked startled. "Christ, no! It's quite a job getting ready to demolish a fifty-million-buck plant that's spread from here to hell-and-gone. The pipeline runs better than a hundred miles, and all swamp."

"When will you be ready?"

"A week . . . maybe less."

"How long will it take to destroy the works after you're ready?" Stark pursued.

"An hour or two at the most," Hawker promised. "We have a master ignition system laid out. One punch on the plunger and you'll see more hell around here than you ever did at Pearl Harbor."

Stark doubted that but didn't say so. However, the words bolstered his confidence in the job that had to be done. He'd seen other men of the same breed; they usually produced.

Hawker continued, "Personally, I hate to see it happen. I've got a lot of my life tied up here—some pretty damned hard-working, sweaty years. I've watched this place grow from a hole in the jungles." He flung his arm reminiscently toward the compound.

"Rough," Stark murmured.

"Hell, yes, it's rough, but I suppose it can't be helped. From what I hear, we haven't the chance of a virgin in sailor town. They say the main Jap fleet is streaming down from the Philippines like sardines." He stared tentatively at the ONI man.

"Maybe so, but the orders are to wait until the last possible moment." Stark smiled grimly. "How would you like to destroy a fifty-million-dollar plant and then have the island hold?"

Hawker laughed boisterously. "Damned if I wouldn't have to get another job."

"Uh-huh, me too."

Hawker banged the desk and bellowed, "Boy . . . beer!"

A scurrying came from the other side of the door and a barefooted Javanese servant clad in a sarong carried in a tray containing the beer and glasses. He placed it on the desk and waited respectfully.

"Get out," Hawker thundered. As the servant wheeled and disappeared, he winked. "You've got to talk that way." he explained. "Treat 'em polite and your name's mud."

"Has he been listening all the time?" Stark asked casually.

"Hell, yes, he has. Them gooks are all ears," he replied. "Obak—that's my houseboy there—knows more about what's going on than I do."

"Maybe too much," Stark suggested gently.

The superintendent smiled meaningfully. "I get the low-down, Mr. Stark, and that's what it takes to run this business. I know every fact from the details about Hodges' nympho wife to exactly how many drops of oil come from each well and, believe me, that's important."

"Who's Hodges?"

"My assistant . . . a damned drunk," he complained. "I would've replaced him a long time ago except the next

13

one probably wouldn't be any better. White men don't last long out here. White women neither." He gulped the beer and continued: "This war's scared him silly. He'd take off now if he could, only he can't. Not till I give the word, and that won't happen till we blow the works."

"How about the natives—any trouble there?"

"None to speak of." He didn't explain the statement.

"Much white help?" Stark asked.

"A few Texans and Oklahomans as field supervisors. They're about the only people who know anything about oil," he explained. Stark nodded politely, thinking the beer tasted good. "We've also got a white doctor, fellow named Ebell," Hawker added.

"American?"

Hawker nodded. "From 'Frisco. He came out here six or eight years ago after his wife died. His daughter's with him now. She came last year."

"How old?"

"Old enough." Hawker smiled evilly. "Don't get your hopes up. We've all tried and failed—she's colder than an iceberg."

Stark thought he could see why but refrained from saying so. He'd seen other so-called icebergs—had watched them melt. Like Elena, whom he'd met in London a few years before while a junior member of a military mission. Tall and cool and composed, she, too, had been an iceberg, or so several of his fellow officers had informed him. He had probed the iceberg, read its message. Tall and cool and composed, but the thaw had been something to remember.

The superintendent gulped the last of his beer. "You might as well meet the wife, then we'll have a look around." He pushed back his chair and stood up. "You'd better not ask too many questions. You're supposed to be an oil man."

"Don't worry, I'm not *sinkeh,*" Stark answered. The native word for "newcomer" brought a startled glance.

"You've been in this neighborhood before," Hawker accused.

14

"Some." The ONI man's face remained blank.

Hawker grunted, then led him through a door into the main part of the house. A number of rattan long chairs were casually grouped near several couches placed to catch any stray breezes from a large overhead fan which, at the moment, Obak was operating by means of a pull rope. A variety of woven mats and Oriental rugs covered the hardwood flooring. Four swinging copper lamps, each of a different size and shape, hung in the corners. He traced the pungent odor of incense to some green candles burning atop a writing desk in one corner.

A stir came from one end of the room and a native woman arose from a couch to meet them. Stark caught the impression of a slender figure clad in white; smooth, even Oriental features framed by a net of abundant black hair before Hawker said, "Selinda, my wife." Hawker glanced at the ONI man, nodding. "This is Mr. Stark . . . of the head office."

"How do you do, Mr. Stark." He acknowledged her greeting with a smile, momentarily speechless and feeling a trifle gauche. Her body might be Oriental, he reflected, but her manner and speech were very much European.

"We weren't expecting you," she was saying.

"The war . . . schedules," he murmured.

"Oh, I know." Her face was slender, almost doll-like, and he found himself thinking she was very beautiful.

"You have a pleasant home," he added.

"But not as nice as home." She smiled demurely. "Care for a drink?"

"No, thank you. Just had one," he replied gravely.

They chatted for a few minutes before Hawker said, "Have a seat; I'll be right back."

He walked toward a kitchen visible in the rear and Stark glanced around, waiting until she settled into a long chair before sitting on one of the couches.

"Will you be here long?" she asked.

A closer glance told him she was not a full-blooded Malay. Although face and figure were Oriental, she had the unmistakable impression of European.

15

Weighing his answer, he decided to take a plunge. "I don't know. I'm really trying to get some information." He stopped, waiting, watching her face.

"About the field? I think it's terrible it has to go," she said. "Mike has worked so hard to build it up."

"I'm sure he has." The use of her husband's given name did not escape him, reinforcing his belief she was not entirely Malay. He added slowly, "Yes, of course, I'm interested in the preparations being made in case the Japanese land. Your husband tells me he has that well in hand."

"He's been working around the clock," she answered. "All the men have."

He watched her levelly. "I'm also trying to run down a little information on Driscoll—find out what happened. The company's interested."

"It was a terrible thing," she murmured. "So young, too."

"Would you know any reason for it?"

"For his death?"

"His murder," he corrected bluntly.

"No, of course not."

"I thought you might have heard rumors," he amended.

"No, I'm sorry. It's just something that none of us could understand."

His eyes searched her face. "Have you ever heard of man named Saito, Mrs. Hawker?"

"Saito . . . it's quite a common Japanese name."

"Saito the Shadow," he pursued deliberately, his senses alert for the slightest change of expression, tone or body reaction.

"Shadow?" She raised her eyes questioningly. "No, I can't say that I have, but it sounds intriguing."

He thought it curious Driscoll should have questioned Hawker on the point and not his wife. She watched him through half-veiled eyes. A girl in Shanghai named Anna Sing Kai had the same smoldering glance; he wondered if Hawker's wife had the same passion. He masked his thoughts.

16

"Have you ever heard of anyone around Palembang by that name?" he asked.

"No, I really haven't." Her face lit up in a smile. "It sounds dreadfully important." Suddenly he became aware Hawker had re-entered the room.

"What the hell would she know about that cloak-and-dagger stuff?" the superintendent snapped. Irked, Stark decided. He filed the information.

"Cloak - and - dagger — it sounds exciting," Selinda Hawker declared. "And I always thought the company such a dull place." He caught the amusement in her voice.

"Let's take a look around," Hawker interrupted. "I've got some work to clean up but you might like to talk to the Doc in the meantime."

"Happy to." Stark arose as the superintendent turned to his wife.

"Have Obak prepare the guest room."

She nodded without taking her eyes from Stark's face and declared, "We'll do our best to make you feel at home, Mr. Stark."

"Thank you, Mrs. Hawker." He cast another glance at her, then followed her husband from the house. A giant black-bearded Bengali got up from the stairs, waiting respectfully while they descended. He stood a good four inches over Stark's six-foot-plus height.

"Who's he?" Stark asked after they were past.

"Gurko Singh, one of the servants," Hawker replied disinterestedly.

"House servant?"

"Sort of, but I generally use him to chauffeur me around the field." Hawker grinned. "He also makes a pretty good bodyguard."

"I can see that," Stark wryly admitted.

When Hawker paused to light his pipe, Stark studied his surroundings. The superintendent's house had a high, steep roof of palm leaves with a surrounding veranda protected from the sun by thick bamboo laths, strung so close together they formed an almost solid screen. The latter interested him. If Driscoll had been murdered on the

17

veranda, as claimed, the killer must have hidden on the porch. Whoever he was, he certainly wasn't a stranger to the household, he decided. The yard was bordered by a bamboo hedge which gave the house an aura of privacy. Palms and senna trees provided shade for several swings set among them.

"That's the infirmary across the way," Hawker stated, motioning toward a long, thatch-roofed building set under some shade trees. "The Doc and his gal have quarters in the rear.

Stark asked her name.

"Suzanne . . . Suzanne Ebell, a real looker."

"Any other help?"

"A nurse . . . Yoshi Kusaka, and a couple of cleanup boys."

"Japanese?"

"Yoshi? Of course." The superintendent cast a quick glance at him. "Just don't get any ideas."

"Because she's Japanese?"

Hawker stopped and faced him squarely. "That's about the size of it, but I can vouch for her. So can Dr. Ebell, or almost anyone else on the compound." His voice softened. "Believe me, if you'd ever see her working through some of these fever sieges we get occasionally you would know what I mean. She's kept that place open when me and the Doc and everyone else was flat on our backs. Yes, sir, I'll vouch for her."

"No need to," Stark answered complacently. "Personally I don't give a damn about her nationality."

Hawker grunted before starting toward the infirmary again. A slender, graying man emerged from an adjoining room as they entered and looked quizzically at them. A quick smile creased his thin face.

"This is Dr. Ebell," Hawker announced. He nodded toward his companion. "Mr. Stark, of the home office." Stark placed the doctor's age at around fifty as they shook hands.

"Glad to have you with us, Stark. Be here long?"

"I don't know," he replied truthfully.

18

"Neither do we." The doctor laughed quickly.

"If you don't mind, I'll leave you two together while I check with Hodges," Hawker cut in. "He can fill you in."

"Not at all," Stark answered, grateful for a chance to talk alone with the man.

"I'll be back pretty quick." The superintendent nodded briefly and left.

Ebell's eyes followed him down the walk. "Mike's got a pretty nasty job on his hands," he explained.

"Oh . . . ?"

"Destroying the plant. He's spent twelve years watching it grow; now they're asking him to blow it up. It's like cutting off his arm."

"It's tough, but it has to be done," Stark observed. "We can't let the Japanese get the oil."

"No, we can't." Ebell glanced around the room. "I feel the same about my little hospital here. It's not much as hospitals go but I've gotten pretty fond of it."

"It'll be waiting, Doctor. This war won't last forever," Stark encouraged.

"No, I don't believe that, Mr. Stark. Neither do you, I suspect."

"I don't follow you."

"The day of the white man is past in this land. When the war's over, there won't be a place in the sun for us any longer," he observed thoughtfully.

Stark bridled. "The Japanese won't win," he snapped.

"No, of course not."

"Then why—?"

"The Malays," Ebell cut in. "When this thing's over you'll find a new nation here. You can hear the stirrings now. It's only a muted sound but it'll rise to a thunder someday. When it does, it'll sweep through the East Indies like a typhoon. Independence—it's a magic word, Mr. Stark."

"Maybe, if they're ready," he replied, realizing the doctor probably was right.

"They're ready."

19

"Any leaders?" Stark asked conversationally.

"Here and there. I'll have to admit there are more and more signs of unrest—even occasional rebellion." He smiled whimsically. "We like to blame it on the Japanese."

"Why not? It's to their advantage," he said softly.

"The Malay is not looking to the Jap," Ebell countered. "He doesn't want another master, white or yellow. All he wants is his own land, and I think he's getting pretty damned tired of bowing and scraping to outsiders."

"You sympathize with them, Doctor?"

"Yes, I do." His voice held a defiant edge. "I sympathize with the underdog everywhere."

"Yet you work for the company."

"As a doctor," Ebell corrected. "I can do some good here."

Stark changed the conversation. "What do you know about Driscoll?"

The doctor's eyes sharpened as he studied the younger man curiously before answering. "He was murdered, if that's what you mean."

"By a native?"

"We have only the evidence of the method," Ebell carefully pointed out. "Certainly a blowgun points to a native, but who can say for sure? We all have lungs." He smiled faintly. The point wasn't lost to Stark.

"Do you have any suspicions?" he queried.

"No, of course not. Driscoll was a thoroughly likable young man—I was quite shocked."

"Do you know of any enemies he made?"

"I can't imagine any."

"Or any reason for his murder?"

"That neither, Mr. Stark. I'm afraid I can't be of much help." He held the agent's eyes. "The company generally isn't this interested."

"This was murder," Stark pointed out.

"I've seen other murders," Ebell observed. "They usually check them with native constabulary, then dump them in a hole and forget about them."

20

"Even Europeans?"

"Even Europeans," he agreed.

"Do you mind if I ask some questions?"

"Certainly not. Go ahead." Ebell eyed him thoughtfully.

"Have you ever heard of a man named Saito?"

"Driscoll asked that same question," he replied, his voice curious. "I take it the man's an *agent provocateur* of some sort."

"Did Driscoll say that?"

"No, but I sort of get the idea." The doctor smiled faintly.

"What did you tell him?" Stark queried.

"Only that I never heard of the man, other than it's not uncommon as a Japanese name."

Stark said bluntly, "Would you mind if I asked your nurse?"

Ebell looked startled. "Because she's Japanese?"

"Partly that, and also because she might be in a position to hear more from the natives."

"There's absolutely no suspicion attached to her," he declared with conviction.

"I'm sure of that."

The doctor hesitated, then turned and called sharply: "Yoshi!"

A slim Japanese girl in a white uniform glided through the door, pausing expectantly, her eyes going first to Stark, then to Ebell. Instead of a nurse's cap she wore a white comb in her hair. Her dark eyes held a misty, fluid look.

"You called, Doctor?"

"Yes, this is Mr. Stark of our home office. He would like to ask you a few questions." Ebell turned to him. "Miss Kusaka, Mr. Stark."

"I'm sorry to disturb you," Stark apologized. "I'll try to be brief."

"That's quite all right. I was just viewing some cultures." Her voice had a lilt that somehow reminded him of small birds twittering in the morning air. Small and

21

delicate like a statue, he thought, placing her age in the late twenties. Reluctantly he brought his attention back to the unpleasant task at hand.

"Have you ever heard of a man named Saito, Miss Kusaka?"

"Saito, why surely. It's quite common among my people." She watched him quizzically.

"I mean here, in Palembang?"

"No, not here. Should I?"

"Not necessarily. We're just trying to get track of him," Stark explained.

"Because he's Japanese?" she asked softly.

He flushed. "Partly that."

"I'm sure I can't help you, Mr. Stark."

"You have—by not knowing him," he answered. She looked momentarily bewildered and Ebell frowned.

"Is that all?" she asked.

"Yes, and thank you, Miss Kusaka."

"Dr. Ebell. . . ." She turned to the graying physician, her face troubled.

"You may go, Yoshi. I'm sure we won't need you any longer."

"Thank you, Doctor." She inclined her head slightly toward Stark and retreated through the doorway.

"She's got the wrong idea about me," he said mournfully. Beneath the proper uniform he'd caught the rhythm of her body; it reminded him of the flow of water.

"Has she?" Ebell smiled stiffly. "What would you expect?"

A sudden rain blew in. Riding a howling wind, slanting, splashing against the earth, it met Stark just outside the door of the infirmary, drenching him to the skin before he reached Hawker's house. It was not until Obak had shown him to the guest room and he was changing that he remembered—he hadn't met the doctor's daughter.

✿ three

THE HAWKER house was gaily lit.

Colored Chinese lanterns glowed like giant fireflies in the garden and on the veranda, and the yellow light from the four copper ceiling lamps gave the main room a festive air. Selinda Hawker, with the aplomb of a good wife entertaining a VIP from the head office, had quickly arranged a small party in Stark's honor, apologizing for the few guests present.

"Mike couldn't bring everyone we'd like to have meet you. The demolition job," she added, with a touch of regret.

"I understand," he assured her.

"But we have invited a couple from the Royal Dutch." Her dark eyes twinkled. "We also have some pretty girls."

He looked at her steadily. "So I see."

"Unattached," she added. They laughed.

Turning at sight of some newly arrived guests, she casually tucked his arm through hers and steered him toward the newcomers. She explained they were two of her husband's field supervisors, Texas Smith and Pete Holden. After the introductions, she left him stuck with a woman presented to him as Martha Hodges.

". . . So when Jasper talked me into coming out here, he promised it would be only for two years," she was telling him. "That was eight years ago."

"I'm sure he had good reason for staying," he answered politely.

"And what would that be?" Her voice was shrewd.

"Why, you're here," he explained. "That makes it home."

"Blarney, Mr. Stark. She smiled engagingly. Tall and

23

beginning to gray, she had nevertheless managed to retain her youthful figure to an astonishing degree and he found her not unattractive. He guessed her age at a shade over forty. He stared across the room at her husband, a man of middle height, going to fat, with a broad, flushed face and heavy jowls—a man given to excesses, if he guessed right.

She took a sip from her glass and added, "Jasper's just interested in the money. They all are. A man wouldn't stay here otherwise."

"It must have its attractions," he protested.

"The trouble is, by the time he makes it there won't be any time left to enjoy it," she continued wistfully.

"You'll have plenty of time," he answered.

"Can you honestly say that with this war going on?"

"Well, it won't last forever."

"Neither will we, I'm afraid. We're probably too late now." Her voice had become edgy.

"No, I don't think so," he encouraged, his eyes resting momentarily on Gurko Singh. The giant Bengali, standing stiffly near the front door, wore a citron-yellow turban. Obak, his yellow face gleaming, was pulling the fan rope while Tombuk, another Malay brought in for the occasion, dashed around supplying drinks. "If the worst comes to the worst, Hawker has an escape route laid out," he added.

"Oh, sure, up river to Telukbetang, then down to Sunda Strait and across to Java, but I wouldn't want to be the one to take it, Mr. Stark."

"Rough, eh?"

"Very rough," she emphatically agreed. "Let's get another drink."

Later he found himself closeted with Texas Smith and Jasper Hodges. When they began talking shop, Stark let his attention wander, feeling all at once bored. Irritably he thought that aside from a brief introduction to Suzanne Ebell, the doctor's daughter, he'd scarcely exchanged a dozen words with her.

He watched her over Hodges' shoulder—a graceful

24

brunette who wore a stunning white evening gown shorn of ornaments, and at the moment was talking animatedly with her father and a tubby, gray-haired merchant from Palembang whom Stark had met earlier.

The first thing that struck him was her height. She was unusually tall for a woman, with a curvesome body under the white sheath that met his full approval. Her clear complexion and even features added up to perfection, or as near to it as he could desire. Although he couldn't see her eyes, he knew they were gray, very large, calm and lovely and utterly passionless.

Watching her now he decided she was no product of make-up or lotions or artificial props. Suzanne Ebell was the real McCoy. He found himself wondering which was the more beautiful, Hawker's graceful Oriental wife or the tall brunette American girl. East or West?

He again became aware of Smith's voice, this time explaining how the destruction system would work. Thin, wiry, of medium height, his narrow face was dominated by a huge beaked nose which made his eyes appear even smaller than they actually were. As Stark got it, valves would allow the oil to flow into the huge earthen fire walls that surrounded each tank; in turn the floors of these were being mined with fire bombs connected to a central switch in the powerhouse.

"She'll go like a goddamned torch," Smith promised. As someone turned on a phonograph and a wailing song of Hindustan filled the room, Smith grimaced and talked louder.

Over his shoulder Stark saw Mike Hawker and Yoshi talking in a corner. The Japanese girl wore a simple, soft green dress and he thought she appeared quite sophisticated. She held her cocktail glass with just the right negligent air, appearing intent on what her burly companion was saying. Someone moved between them, then Hodges' grating voice broke into his ear.

"I say we ought to blow this thing now and get out while we can. Hawker's plumb crazy. He doesn't know how close the Japs are."

Stark switched his attention back to the assistant superintendent. The latter's speech had become thick, slurred, and his small, piggish eyes danced curiously, as if out of focus. Swilled to the gills, he thought. Hawker was right; the man was a drunk. He wondered if Hawker was also right about Martha Hodges.

"Maybe the Japs can't take the island," Texas Smith cut in.

"Bushwah. What's to stop 'em? A couple of Limey flak guns, a handful of Colonial troops and nothing else. They'll breeze in." Hodges eyed Stark belligerently. "What about it?"

"Hard to say," he replied evasively.

"Let 'em come," Texas Smith snorted. "We'll make this the Alamo in reverse."

Hodges snickered. "Listen to him. He thinks he's Davy Crockett." He gulped the last of his drink and yelled: "Boy, an Irish whiskey."

A moment later Smith excused himself and Hodges turned belligerently to Stark, saying loudly, "I hear you've been making inquiries about Driscoll, the guy that got killed."

Stark stared at the red face. "The company's interested," he replied.

"Hell, people are dying all the time," Hodges retorted callously.

"But not by murder." He coldly watched the other for reaction.

"There's plenty of that, too. Most of these gooks would just as soon slip a knife between your ribs as look at you."

"How about poisoned darts?" Stark demanded, his voice sharp and intent.

"That, too. It's these damned Bataks," Hodges growled.

"Much trouble?" he casually asked.

"Trouble?" Hodges' eyes seemed to dance again. "Of course there's trouble. If it ain't one thing it's another—these damned gooks will knock us all off before they're through."

26

"Still, there'd have to be a reason . . ."

"Reason, hell. Anything serves as a reason in this country. I could tell you plenty—" Whatever he started to say was broken by Selinda's sudden appearance.

"The guest of honor . . . I'm afraid we're neglecting you." She made a mock bow at Hodges. "Mike promised we wouldn't talk business tonight, remember?"

"We were just gossiping," Stark commented.

"And neglecting the girls," she finished.

"Not by choice. Besides—" he smiled—"the prettiest ones are married."

"You, too, Mr. Stark," she demurred severely. "I seem to have heard that line before."

He laughed, at the same time seeing Hodges sneer.

"I have no doubt of that, Mrs. Hawker," he gallantly declared.

"For heaven's sake, call me Selinda."

"And I'm Joe."

Hodges turned abruptly away, and her eyes followed him musingly before turning back.

"All right, Joe." She slipped her arm through his and swung him toward a corner where Tombuk was mixing drinks. "Let's get this show on the road."

Chatting for a while over a couple of gin slings, he idly asked how long she'd lived in Palembang, noting her hesitancy before answering.

"A little over a year," she confessed.

"Oh?" He arched his eyes. "Then you haven't been married long." He made it a statement.

"The same length of time," she admitted. "I met Mike in Singapore. Well . . ." She shrugged.

"And he swept you off your feet," he interjected.

"Something like that." A distant look clouded her face. "I miss it sometimes."

"Singapore?"

"Of course."

"But you're not sorry?" This time she looked gravely at him while he waited, sensing she was considering her answer.

27

"I don't know," she said finally. "At times I think Palembang's at the end of the world."

"It pratically is," he conceded.

She swung toward him and touched his hand. "Anyway, I'm glad you came."

"Why?" he asked, sensing he already knew the answer.

"Because of this." She gestured toward the room. "It's not often we have an excuse for a party, even a quiet one like this."

"Quiet?" he politely asked. Hodges was talking with Pete Holden, one of the field supervisors, and his voice had risen above the sound of the phonograph. She laughed as she caught his meaning.

"You'll have to forgive Jasper," she explained. "Everyone out here has to have an escape. His is drink."

"And his wife's?"

She didn't answer immediately. The suggestion of amusement touched her lips, slowly breaking into a mischievous smile.

"Why don't you ask her?" she challenged.

"I'd rather ask you," Stark told her deliberately.

"About Martha?" Mockery filled her face.

"About you," he pursued. The look left her face.

"I escape, too," she answered simply.

"That sounds interesting."

"Mmmmm . . ." She looked deliciously at him and he was surprised to find himself faintly disturbed and a bit puzzled over the turn the conversation had taken.

He regarded her with new insight; she returned his stare, open-faced, her dark eyes curiously somnolent. When two late guests arrived, a shade of disappointment flicked across her countenance.

She said tonelessly, "The Vandervoorts . . . from the Plaju plant. I'll introduce you."

Stark found himself shaking hands with a portly, middle-aged man who spoke with a thick Dutch accent. The fat woman with him was his wife. Releasing Stark's hand he began apologizing to Selinda for their tardiness, explaining it was due to the preparations for demolishing the plant.

"Poof, the same old excuse," Selinda facetiously exclaimed.

When the Dutchman stopped laughing, Stark asked how the work was progressing. He began explaining that all the plants on the lower Plaju were being mined for simultaneous destruction, but in the middle of the conversation Hawker broke in and called for drinks.

Stark noticed Selinda had withdrawn to talk with Mrs. Vandervoort and Texas Smith at the other side of the room. She glanced toward him and their eyes met briefly before she turned away. Hawker switched the conversation to tiger hunting, a favorite and necessary pastime. Stark listened a few minutes, then excused himself and wandered off, thinking he'd like to get drunk.

The evening had almost passed before he managed to corner Suzanne Ebell alone. Despite Hawker's assertion of her coldness, she'd been the undisputed belle of the ball, seldom without a group of people around her.

He finally caught her between partners, saying, "I'm lonesome."

A brief smile lit her face. "I'm afraid we haven't been taking very good care of you, Mr. Stark." Her eyes appraised him without seeming to.

"Joe's the name," he informed her.

"I like that better," she replied. "I'm Suzanne."

"I know."

"You didn't appear neglected," she accused. So she had noticed! He knew she made reference to the fact that Selinda had kept him in tow for much of the evening.

"Our hostess is too gracious," he murmured. "She felt sorry for me."

"I can't believe that."

He smiled, pleased with the subtle flattery. They made small talk for a while. Seeing her hands empty, he said, "A lost soul; a woman without a drink. Care for one?"

"I wouldn't mind—a gin sling."

29

He smiled slightly. "That seems to be the custom here. Excuse me a moment."

He went to the corner where Tombuk was mixing the drinks, got two and returned. She took a glass from his hand, staring thoughtfully at him.

"You haven't been in the islands long, have you?"

"Why do you say that?" he asked.

"Walking over to get the drinks. The other men would just scream for a boy."

"Don't you approve?"

"Yes, certainly. Personally I think our manners are abominable. I was just surprised." She sipped from her glass and he glanced toward the veranda.

"It's stuffy in here. Would you care to step outside?"

She watched him mischievously over the rim of her glass and murmured, "So soon?"

"We haven't much time," he responded gravely, thinking she was every bit as beautiful as he had conjectured.

The air of lightness left her face, as she answered. "No, we haven't."

He touched her elbow and they turned toward the veranda. Gurko Singh bowed solemnly as they passed through the door. "Let's go into the garden. It's more pleasant."

They passed between a row of glowing Chinese lanterns to the border of flowering shrubs and sat on a lawn swing. The air was warm, still, and a half-moon, moltenly silver, hung in the eastern sky. From somewhere in the distance a tom-tom began thudding a slow, solemn beat, calling the graveyard shift to work. Stark was reminded of tropic nights everywhere—Manila, Palawan, Honolulu, Samoa; it was the same halfway around the world in Panama, Cuba, Bermuda. He was a tropics man, had been since almost the start of his naval career. He had been to a thousand strange places on assignments covering everything from theft of government property to espionage— and murder. Each assignment, each place had brought forth something new; and from each place he had retained a little something, though perhaps sometimes not more than a fleeting memory. He wondered what Sumatra held in store.

Suzanne stirred and he asked, "Cigarette?"

"Thanks, I will." She took one, absently tapping it against her nail. Under the flare of the lighter her face appeared grave and thoughtful. She inhaled briefly, then stared into the eastern sky, murmuring, "It's beautiful here."

"Yes, but I wouldn't have admitted that unitl now," he replied.

She turned toward him. "Sometimes I wonder why I stay, then at times like this I think it's the most beautiful place in the world," she confessed.

"I love the tropic nights," he admitted. It's about all that makes life tolerable."

"You've been here before?" Her voice held faint surprise.

"Not in Palembang, but I've been around a bit." When she didn't answer, he pursued: "Why do you stay?"

"I've told you."

He placed their empty glasses on a lawn table and said, "Not quite. You can fall in love with the tropic nights but there are lots of places better than this—places without poverty and disease."

"I suppose so."

"Then why do you stay?" he urged.

"I don't know. I've asked myself that question . . . many times." She faced him. "On the other hand, I have nothing to go back to—no other family or relatives."

"A beautiful woman always has something to go back to," he answered gruffly.

She didn't reply immediately, but after a moment they began talking about the States, and then her background. He learned she had been raised in San Francisco, where her father had had a private practice until her mother's death, after which he had come to Sumatra Independent to take charge of the company's medical facilities. She had gone to college, had been married briefly—she didn't enlarge on it nor did he ask.

31

In turn, he told her a bit about his early life—school and college in Los Angeles, the dances and beach parties, and of his parents, now dead. He skipped the part about the Naval Academy and glossed over his later life, feeling hypocritical about passing himself off as a company employee.

They were chatting about her father's work when he heard movement and glanced around. A couple came down the walk between the rows of lanterns, cut across the lawn toward them, then halted. He recognized Martha Hodges and Pete Holden, the field supervisor. Their voices came as a low murmur and they moved closer together, locked in a tight embrace, kissing passionately. Suzanne glanced at them and Stark felt her stiffen.

"We'd better return to the veranda," he murmured.

"Yes, it's getting late." They stopped on the veranda, lingering as if each were reluctant to rejoin the party. Stark looked down into her face.

"What do you do here for pastime?"

"Pastime?"

"The favorite sport—some way of having fun," he explained.

"You mean like golf, or tennis?" She looked dubious.

"That's it," he replied enthusiastically.

"Well, this isn't exactly Waikiki Beach," she exclaimed. "Sometimes we row up the river."

"Have you a boat?"

"My father has a small prau."

Stark drew himself up stiffly and made a mock bow from the waist. "Miss Ebell," he said formally, "would you condescend to go boating with me tomorrow? In your father's prau, of course."

She suppressed a giggle. "I'd be delighted, Mr. Stark."

❀ four

HIS EYES suddenly opened.

Shadows filled the room, broken by pale beams that filtered through the bamboo shades. Stark didn't know how long he'd slept, or what had awakened him, but only that he'd been jerked to sudden consciousness. He lay for a moment listening, groping with his thoughts, then remembered the party.

Jasper Hodges had gotten into a boisterous argument with his wife and had stumbled against a table smashing one of Selinka Hawker's beautiful Chinese lanterns. He had vented his drunken rage by slugging Obak, until Hawker and Texas Smith had interceded, leading him outside while Martha apologized for his behavior. After that the party broke up.

Stark had walked Suzanne back to her quarters, but by then the gaiety of the evening had fled and they said goodnight briefly, although not before he reminded her of the promise to go boating.

A faint shuffling came from the veranda outside his door and abruptly he sat up, feeling his heart rise to a rapid beat. Someone on the porch! A hissing came from beyond the door and it took him a second to recognize the sound as a human voice. He sat, suddenly still, staring at the shafts of moonlight filtering between the laths; beyond he discerned movement.

"*Tuan* . . . " The whisper came, followed by a surreptitious scratching at the window that reminded him of the paw of an animal.

He silently moved from bed, pulled on his trousers, then remembering Driscoll's fate, got a .45-caliber automatic from his traveling bag and shoved it into his waistband. Moving to one side of the door, he edged back the shade and studied the veranda. Aside from the shadow next to the door he saw no one.

"*Tuan* . . . " The low whisper came, borne on a note of urgency.

Pulling the door ajar, Stark saw the slim form of a Malay. He kept his eyes on the man's hands and moved carefully into the opening.

"What is it?" he demanded tersely.

"Tuan come . . . Tuan come." The Malay gestured toward the river.

Stark sensed the fear in his voice. A trick? He studied him through half-lidded eyes, thinking there was nothing toward the river—nothing but small clearings of lalang grass set amid jungled thickets. Swamps and trees and beasts. He'd be damned . . .

"Who sent you?" he demanded.

The man recoiled, frightened, then spoke pleadingly: "Tuan come."

Stark took another step forward. "What is this? Speak up, man!" Cringing, the Malay remained silent. Stark lowered his voice. "What's the matter—don't you understand me?"

The Malay shook his head violently.

"*Tuan* come," he repeated. He seemed to struggle with his thoughts before adding: "Driscoll."

"Driscoll!" Stark exclaimed. "What do you know about him?"

The native retreated to the edge of the porch as if frightened and for an instant Stark feared he would flee. Driscoll—the name of the dead agent rang in his mind.

"Wait . . . one moment," he commanded tersely.

Retreating into the room, he quickly finished dressing and moved the automatic to his jacket pocket, then scanned the veranda through the window again and went onto the porch.

The moon was falling into the west, casting great slanting beams that turned the landscape to a milky white. The Malay hovered near the steps, waiting. Seeing Stark, he

34

turned without a word and hurried through the yard, then plunged toward the river.

Stark followed, trying to keep him in sight and at the same time watch both sides of the path. No sooner had the darkness closed around him than he realized his foolishness. Right now he was set up for the plucking. *An agent's first mistake usually is his last.* That's what Durling always claimed. He could see the Old Man now, shaking his head disapprovingly. Well, to hell with it.

The slim figure became a shadowy blur ahead and Stark hurried to catch up, realizing the pursued man was running just fast enough to maintain an even distance between them. The Malay crossed the border of the compound without looking back. Before reaching the river he turned into a series of small clearings that ran through the jungled thickets like a string of sickly yellow beads.

Stark tried to organize his thoughts as he followed. Trap—it had all the earmarks. The native was cagey; he hadn't given him a chance to ask questions. Instead he had sucked him into following by use of the dead agent's name, bait he must have known he couldn't resist. No, that was wrong—the Malay wouldn't know that. He was merely a messenger, but for whom? Saito? Driscoll's killer? Or were they one and the same? Well, he'd find out.

He called softly but the Malay only increased his gait. Swearing, Stark moved faster, realizing that the familiar compound was now far behind. He yelled louder.

The Malay sped along a path winding through waist-hig lalang grass and vanished into the trees at the opposite side. Sweat coursed down Stark's face and his breath came in labored gasps but he pushed doggedly ahead. Plunging into the border of trees, he pushed ahead a dozen yards and abruptly stopped, listening.

The bright chirrup of cicadas, the murmur of water and somewhere the twitter of birds were all that broke the silence. No sound came from the dark trail ahead. He peered into the blackness, waiting, feeling his heart thud against his chest.

Withdrawing the automatic, he flicked off the safety and

held the weapon loosely at his waist, all his senses attuned to the night while he waited for the trap to close. His eyes searched around him. The forest was a thing of many parts—impenetrable thickets, monkeys, giant pythons, shadows, stillness, black pieces of water.

When the Malay didn't return after a moment, he knew he'd been led on a wild-goose chase. He fingered the automatic and felt his body grow cold. What kind of a trap? Not the deadly dart of a blowgun certainly. That could have been arranged in an easier fashion. But why this? The answer came in a flash of insight: he had to be killed without it appearing like murder! Die here and his body would never be found. Whatever the answer, he wouldn't die like Driscoll. He savagely shook his head— he wouldn't die at all.

He began to edge back toward the clearing while scanning the jungle around him. The night seemed all at once hostile. Moonbeams filtering through the trees painted eerie shadows on the sodden floor and the musky scent of decay filled his nostrils. He heard small rustlings, twittering noises, the low murmur of water somewhere off to his right. That would be the river. An odd memory of standing in another jungle somewhere flicked through his mind and as quickly vanished, leaving him alone with his fears. His heart seemed to be pounding abnormally loud.

Suddenly a nerve-chilling scent filled his nostrils and something prickled at his memory. *Tiger!* The name leaped from his subconscious and with it the memory of the scent from another time, in Rangoon.

He stood absolutely still and tried to determine the direction from which it came. The air lay hot and muggy, pressing against his body like a damp blanket. He stilled his fears. *Retreat, boy, you're in a bad spot,* he told himself.

Stark swung his head slowly around, testing the night. The scent diminished somewhat and he continued edging toward the clearing, a few nerve-racking steps at a time.

The Malay jungles held many things—elephants, tapirs, bears and the one- and two-horned rhinos, but nothing so fearful as the tiger. The knowledge didn't reassure him.

Reaching the clearing, he caught movement at the edge of his eye and swung his head; it took several seconds to realize he was watching the Malay race back toward the compound.

The native had tricked him neatly. He had cut through the jungle just long enough to lose him, and now was backtracking at top speed. Suckered, he thought sourly. He started to shout, then remembered the tiger and chopped off the words. The thought clung to his mind that whoever had sent the Malay was a person of power —enough power to force the native to lead him into the trap. The man's fear proved that.

The scent came again, suddenly stronger, assailing his nostrils with a sickening, musky odor, pungent, yet with the unmistakable tang of carrion. Fancying he saw the .lalang grass bending, he took a backward step.

Something scurried toward him and he jerked up the automatic, at the same time hearing a high squeal. Hesitating, he glanced around and resolutely took a few steps forward, catching sight of a small pig tethered to a stake. He stood for several seconds, nervously watching and straining to hear. What sounds did a tiger make in the night? The pig was the bait—or rather he was, he thought.

The animal had been staked there to bring the tiger to the scene. In turn, he had been lured to the same rendezvous. He'd been shot, knifed, bludgeoned, had faced death in many ways—but never this. He smiled grimly, wondering what the Old Man would do in the same situation.

Despite the danger he slipped forward and released the animal. Squealing, it dashed into the high grass. The thought flashed through his mind that the pig knew where the tiger was, fleeing to safety. He stifled the urge to follow, reluctant to leave the border of trees. His fear told him to get back to the compound as quickly as possible but judgment restrained him. The tiger lay somewhere close, lurking in the tall lalang grass, perhaps waiting for him to make the wrong move. Yellow eyes seemed to bore into him.

The scent became stronger and his nerves tightened, growing edgy. The automatic became wet with sweat. Wiping his face on his sleeve, he stepped to the side of the nearest tree. The vile scent permeated the motionless air.

He started to put the automatic in his pocket and clamber up the tree when a hideous snarl broke from the grass. It parted and he saw a vicious yellow head. The snarl came again. Ears flattened and head lowered, the tiger watched him. He yanked up the weapon, took a quick aim and fired just as it leaped.

The weapon recoiled and he twisted, throwing his body behind the shelter of the tree trunk. The cat sailed past and he got in two more shots at less than a yard's distance. The animal struck the ground, thrashed for a few seconds and whirled again, crouching and watching him with baleful eyes. His long tail switched angrily. The ludicrous thought flashed through Stark's mind that tigers simply didn't come this large.

It moved suddenly to one side as if it recognized the barrier of the tree and he edged farther around it. The big cat lowered its head and he took aim again.

Wham! The weapon blasted into the night as the cat took a sudden step forward. Wham! Wham! Something yellow sailed through the air, snarling, and a hot iron raked his forearm as the cat shot past. Desperately he leaped after it and managed to jam the weapon into its head, firing just as it whirled. He pulled the trigger several more times, hearing the empty click. The thing was thrashing on the ground almost at his feet and turning, he dropped the gun and pulled himself into the tree.

A dozen feet above the ground he stopped climbing and clung to a branch, panting. His hands shook and sweat stung his eyes. The thrashing below him stopped and finally he moved down several feet, then pushed the branches apart. A tawny yellow body lay at the edge of

38

the plain, motionless under the moon. His arm ached and he felt blood dripping from his fingers.

Gingerly he clambered down to the plain, searching until he found the automatic. Taking a last look at the dead cat, he started toward the compound but almost as quickly stopped. Someone yelled in the distance and he saw a flaring torch. He groped for a clip, found none and waited, watching the torch draw nearer in a jogging motion. A giant form seemed to emerge from the night like magic, with the moonlight caught and reflected from a wavy kris.

"Here," Stark yelled. His voice sounded unnatural, hoarse. An instant later he recognized the torch-bearer as Gurko Singh. The giant Bengali came to a halt before him.

"Tuan!" He glanced worriedly around before spotting the tiger. When he did, his eyes held it for a moment, then swung back to Stark with an expression akin to reverence.

"La illah il Allah," he exclaimed softly. His eyes fixed Stark's and he bowed humbly, saying, "I come too late, tuan."

"Nasty," Dr. Ebell exclaimed. Gurko Singh had awakened him in his quarters at the rear of the infirmary and now he stood swabbing the blood from Stark's arm with a wad of sterile cotton. He had thrown on an old bathrobe over his pajamas and his feet were shoved into a pair of native sandals. His face looked gaunt and tired as he stepped back to adjust the lamp. "I must say, you're my first tiger victim."

Stark's arm throbbed, burning as if from a hot iron. The shock of the encounter had passed but he felt weak from loss of blood and a trifle dizzy. Managing a smile, he said, "I thought that was quite a common occurrence around here." He clenched his fist while Ebell probed at the wound.

"So it is," Ebell agreed. "The big cats take a terrible toll. You just happen to be the first victim that got away alive." He glanced curiously at him.

Stark started to reply when Suzanne hurried through

39

the door, a wrap thrown over her nightgown and her dark hair disheveled. She caught her breath at sight of him and he winked reassuringly.

"What happened?" she asked, her features immediately registering anxiety.

"Tiger," her father answered, without looking around.

"Tiger!" she exclaimed disbelievingly, then hurried around to see Stark's arm, involuntarily gasping at sight of it.

"Not too bad," Ebell reassured. Stark gritted his teeth as the doctor cleaned and swabbed the wounds with an antiseptic.

"The bones and muscles seem to have escaped," he added with satisfaction. A few stitches and a tetanus shot and you'll be as good as new. Of course, it will be quite sore for a few days."

"Dreadful," Suzanne murmured, looking worriedly at Stark.

"Not half so bad as it could have been. That cat looked pretty hungry to me."

"How did it happen?" She searched his face, seeming to have regained her composure.

He hesitated, aware her father had paused to listen, then briefly related the story.

When he finished, Ebell whistled softly and asked, "Would you recognize the native?"

"Probably not. I never got a very good look at him." He smiled sourly. "Most Malays look pretty much alike, at least to a newcomer."

"How would he—" Suzanne stopped, biting her lip and watching him curiously.

He returned the look gravely. "That's just it. It had to be someone pretty well acquainted with the Hawker household, at least well enough to know my room. But that isn't the point."

The doctor eyed him curiously. "What is the point?"

"Who the real murderer is,'" Stark replied slowly. "The Malay was just a tool. He was as scared out there as I was. The man I'm after is the man who sent him."

"Murder . . ." Ebell uttered slowly, glancing hard at the ONI man. "You think this is related to the Driscoll case?"

"What else?"

Suzanne stirred suddenly, declaring, "So do I. Things like this just don't happen. A tiger trap!" She shuddered and her face became fearful. "But why you?"

"Yes, I suppose you're right," her father agreed, disregarding the question, "but it's not a pleasant thing to contemplate." He sighed heavily and resumed work.

Stark debated asking about Yoshi, curious whether or not anyone had heard her leaving her quarters during the night, but decided against it. Ebell had already aired his opinion on that score and would be apt to consider any further questioning as persecution. He had little doubt Suzanne felt the same about it. Instead he joked, "Just when I had a date to go boating with a pretty girl, too."

"No boating for you, Mr. Stark," she replied severely.

"Maybe we could just sit in the prau and talk," he suggested. "I think I'd like that better. Besides, this will call for a period of recuperation, with a pretty nurse of course."

"Yoshi will be busy," she murmured.

"Yoshi—who's talking about Yoshi?" He flinched as the needle bit into his arm.

Suzanne spoke, troubled again. "I'd suggest you stay on the compound, at least until we find out what this is all about."

"Sure, Driscoll got it right on the veranda," he pointed out.

"For heaven's sake, Joe, be serious," she exclaimed.

"I am serious. A dart's just as fatal as a tiger."

"And easier to come by," Ebell added cynically.

"Gurko Singh was very brave," she said suddenly. "The natives are dreadfully afraid of that area, even during the day. That's what they call it—the tiger field."

They remained silent until the arm was dressed, then Ebell observed: "I'd better have a look at it tomorrow.

41

We don't want to take a chance on infection. Cigarette?" He produced a pack and they both took one.

Ebell studied him thoughtfully while they lit up but didn't say anything. They smoked for a moment in silence and watching Suzanne, Stark thought the night had been almost worth it. He wondered if she'd read his mind for she suddenly flushed as if just aware she wore but a thin wrap over her nightgown. He suppressed a grin of admiration.

Not seeming to have noticed the byplay, Ebell stated, "Well, that about winds it up. Now you'd better try to get some sleep."

"And no more tiger hunting," she added severely.

"Don't worry, from now on I stick with the praus," he told her.

Thanking the doctor, he bade them both good night. As he left the dispensary, Gurko Singh rose from beside the door and followed him to the house, where he lay down on the veranda outside his door to sleep.

Stark slept better for that fact.

❀ five

THE JAPANESE planes came over that evening.

Stark had gone to the infirmary earlier to get his arm dressed, a task performed by Yoshi since Dr. Ebell was in the field. She worked quickly, professionally, with scarcely a word, nor did either of them make reference to their earlier conversation.

He watched her with mixed feelings, wondering if she were as innocent as she seemed. He wished he knew. Finished, she nodded and quickly turned to a Malay waiting with an ulcerated leg. Stark left the infirmary feeling like a schoolboy caught in some prank. He had spent the afternoon resting and fretting from inactivity.

Now he was sitting with Suzanne in a corner of the garden. The sun, a fantastically bright golden ball, balanced on the western horizon and a hot breeze stirred the trees. They had been discussing her father's work when he happened to lift his eyes.

It was then he saw the aircraft. They came out of the southwest, three glittering specks caught in the long rays of the sun.

Suzanne saw him stiffen and quickly asked, "What is it?"

"Planes." He uttered the single word, watching the sky. They came swiftly, dropping as they flew over the Plaju River refineries, heading straight toward Sumatra Independent.

"Japanese?" she asked worriedly.

"Probably." He'd scarcely spoken before they zoomed past, displaying the meatball insignia on their wings. "Zeros, probably carrier-based," he added harshly.

"Oh." Her voice was very small.

"Don't worry, they're just looking the place over," he assured her. "They want the plant intact."

Hodges ran from the office and stared at the vanishing aircraft. Stark smiled mirthlessly. Well, this would make him sweat. He pushed the man from his mind and returned his attention to the sky. The planes swung toward the north, the thunder of their engines dying away as they vanished over the crown of trees.

"Do you think it'll be long?" Suzanne tremulously asked.

He looked down into her face. She was watching him, worriedly, and desperately he wanted to kiss her. Instead he replied, "No, I don't."

"Maybe Hodges is right—maybe we should have gone while there was time."

"Afraid?" he asked softly.

"I don't know." She turned and stared over the jungle.

43

"Sometimes this seems like a bad dream and I wonder when I'll awake and there won't be any Sumatra—no jungle or heat or death. No war. I'll just suddenly find myself in the Cliff House watching the tides roll through the Golden Gate." She turned toward him. "I know that's silly but that's the way I feel."

Stark kissed her then. He did it simply and tenderly, a soft meeting of their lips which at first was little more than a light caress. He finally moved his head away.

"I've wanted to do that since the first night," he confessed.

She regarded him with a light he hadn't seen in her eyes before; when she spoke, the words came so softly he could scarcely hear them. "Then why didn't you?"

He kissed her again, longer, and this time felt her respond—felt it in her lips and body and the pressure of her hands against his back. He clung to her with mixed feelings of tenderness and elation. She trembled against him. When they broke apart she stepped back, clinging to his hands.

"Joe . . ."

"What is it?" he gently asked.

"I'm scared now, Joe."

"Don't be."

"But there's not much time . . . not much time."

"Time enough."

He drew her close, holding and sensing her, content to feel the softness of her hair against his face, and it seemed to him he had known her a long time. He didn't know how long they stood that way, but suddenly the balancing sun had gone and with it the great shaft of splaying yellow light which had flooded the garden. They turned and he saw Gurko Singh standing on the veranda; the Bengali stared into the darkening sky.

"Let's walk," Suzanne murmured.

"Let's," he agreed huskily.

She caught his hand and they turned toward the river, strolling wordlessly while the dusk came speeding in and the stars popped out, one by one, glowing fluidly in the sky. Her white face became a pale blur. They stopped under a tulip tree and kissed again, more fervently this time until finally she broke away.

"Joe . . . ?"

"What is it?" he asked, aware his blood was racing; his heart sang and he felt high. Suzanne watched him without reply and he sensed her thoughts.

In scarcely more than a whisper, she said, "Time is running out."

"Hush, honey."

"I know. I feel it and it scares me. We're not even sure of tomorrow."

"Don't be scared." He kissed her lips and eyes, then held her close. She moved tightly into the circle of his arms and pressed against him, pulling herself to him, trembling. He moved his hands slowly over her body.

"Joe, we've got to stop this." She pushed away, staring at him. "I don't know what you must think of me."

"I think you're the most wonderful thing that ever happened to me."

"I don't know what's getting into me." She laughed nervously. "Maybe it's this magic of the tropics you mentioned."

"Whatever it is, I like it."

She caught his hand again. "So do I. Let's walk."

They turned back from the river and wandered aimlessly, sensing the warmth of the night. Stark knew the trouble in her mind for he had sensed the battle she was waging within herself when she murmured: *Time is running out.* He was content.

The moon rode in the east, washing the landscape, and in its pale light he caught the strained, taut look on Suzanne's face. Yet she looked more beautiful than ever, more desirable. Her body was long and supple, rounded as it should be, exquisitely molded as few were. He felt his pulse quicken. As the rear of the infirmary loomed up, he stared at it in dismay, fearful the night was about to end. Passing the small house where Yoshi lived, they

45

came to another and she stopped abruptly, then swung to face him. She tried to speak but the words wouldn't come.

"Say what you have to say," he urged.

"I don't know. . . ." She moved to the door and he followed. Opening it, she turned to face him.

"Joe, kiss me and go."

He kissed her hard, holding her tightly. His lips caressed her face and eyes while his hands found her body —it was strong, vibrant, a symphony of curves and planes. She strained against him, then suddenly pushed him away.

"You've got to go," she whispered. She moved backward through the doorway without taking her eyes from him, and he followed, closing the door behind him. The room was dark, broken only by the pale light which filtered through the windows from the moon- and star-washed skies.

"Where's your father?" he abruptly asked.

"In the field." She spoke tonelessly.

"Suzanne . . ."

"You've got to go," she implored. "I'm not made of steel; I'm made of flesh and blood."

"So am I."

"You've got to go. . . ."

She stopped speaking, swaying slightly, and took a step toward him. He caught her to him and kissed her, hard at first and then more gently. She struggled briefly, fighting herself as well as him, but then she began returning his embraces, her breath passionate in his ear. He felt his pulses race, the surge of blood, his hand found her breasts while he murmured endearments.

She moaned softly, and suddenly pulled away, fumbling with her dress. She moved through a doorway; he hesitated and followed. It was a small room—a bureau, dressing screen, bed, chair; the fragrance of a subtle perfume and drapes at the window told him it was hers. She came out from behind the screen, her body a pale blur.

"Joe . . . Joe," she whispered. Her hands were at her sides, palms outward, beseeching. For just an instant he stared. Her legs were long, graceful, her stomach flat.

46

He moved his eyes up, caught hers. The floodtide broke. He stepped forward, kissed her brutally—she returned his fervor. Her breasts were large, firm, taut-nippled, and he caressed her hungrily, pushing her to a sitting position on the edge of the bed.

"Oh God, Joe," she murmured, bringing his head down so he could kiss the nipples of her breasts. Her body quivered and surged hotly against him. Slowly, then, she sank back, slipping her arms around him, pulling him down on top of her. Her naked flesh was warm and vibrant and receptive to the demands of his hard, pulsing maleness. She held him tight, her pelvis working convulsively, her mouth linked with his, seeking passionate union with him as the stars seemed to explode all around them.

✿ SIX

THE WAR came suddenly nearer.

Radio Australia reported the Japanese had reinforced their new beachheads at Rabaul in New Britain and Kavieng on New Ireland. On the northeast coast of New Guinea, Lae and Salamau were under heavy attack and another powerful enemy task force was moving toward Port Darwin, the Allied stronghold on Australia's northeast coast.

Japanese naval units had steamed into Staring Bay on one of the near-by Celebes Islands and Borneo had been assaulted by land, sea and air. A number of Japanese reconnaissance planes had flown over Palembang and the Dutch harbormaster reported the gray forms of naval units lurking in Bangka Strait. Clearly a noose had been drawn around Sumatra.

Mike Hawker called an immediate council of war. Besides Stark it included Jasper Hodges, Texas Smith and

Pete Holden, the latter two in charge of laying the demolitions. Dr. Ebell had been included to take care of any medical questions. Hawker posted Gurko Singh at the door with orders to allow no one to enter. When they were settled, he announced without preamble:

"Vandervoort phoned that the Plaju River refineries are about ready to blow the works. He says an assault is imminent. Now it's up to us; we have to make a fast decision." His agate eyes swept the circle of faces before he continued. "I realize this is my decision and mine alone, but I'd like to get your thinking." His eyes settled on Stark.

"But they won't start until the Japs actually land." Stark made it a statement.

"No, they won't."

"Then we've got to wait."

Hawker nodded agreement and turned to Hodges.

"I say blow it," his assistant declared vehemently. He dug at his grimy nails with a penknife as he spoke. "We know damned well they're coming and we haven't got the chance of a snowball in hell. We knew that when they knocked off the *Repulse* and *Prince of Wales*." . . . .

He stared belligerently at the ONI man, who returned it stonily. Hawker made no comments but instead turned toward Texas Smith.

"Let's wait," the latter drawled laconically.

"How about you, Holden?" Hawker asked tersely.

Stark looked at the driller, a tall, gangling man with a narrow weather-beaten face. He lit a cigarette before answering. "I say let's wait until we see the yellow bastards."

"By that time you'll be dead," Hodges gritted.

"We can't afford to blow a fifty-million-buck plant and then not have them come," he replied. He smiled humorlessly. "The company wouldn't like that."

"No, it wouldn't," Hawker agreed.

They talked about the general situation for a while. Holden thought the Japs might have a hard time fording the river due to the downstream troops. Hawker dissented,

48

pointing out that if they struck, they'd employ sufficient force to assure quick victory. Stark felt inclined to agree with him. He noticed Ebell didn't join the conversation, nor was he asked. A lull came while they lit cigarettes and got beer, then Hodges made another pitch for destroying the refineries immediately. Hawker eyed him thoughtfully while he talked, but it was Texas Smith who answered him.

"The point is, we're still loading oil down at the docks, and we need every drop we can get out. Besides, we have a margin of safety."

"What margin?" Hodges asked nastily.

"They'll have to hit the other refineries first. That'll give us lead time," he replied imperturbably.

Hodges flushed and retorted bitterly, "We've got our families to think of—at least some of us have."

"Families don't count," Hawker stated coolly. "How close are we to being finished?" He addressed the question to Texas Smith.

The field supervisor stared at the ceiling. "Most of it's ready to go now," he explained. "We're still laying demolitions under the jungle pipelines and we have a few spots in the compound left to cover. Nothing much to speak of."

"That pipeline's important," Hawker pointed out.

"Sure, the Japs couldn't operate without it," Smith assented, "but don't worry—we're getting it."

"Well, that about wraps it up." The superintendent rapped his knuckles against the desk and glanced around. "We'll hold until they blow the Royal Dutch, then go to work. In the meantime, push ahead with that damned pipeline."

"I'd like to raise a point," Stark said quietly.

"Shoot." Hawker eyed him.

"I take it the powerhouse is the key—the location of the central demolition switches."

"Correct," the superintendent agreed.

"I think we should keep a man there around the clock. Not a Malay," he added.

49

"Talo's absolutely trustworthy," Holden cut in.

Texas Smith, watching the ONI man through hooded eyes, removed his cigarette and said, "I agree with Stark."

"What the hell's wrong with Talo?" Hodges cut in.

"He might be the *mandur* but he's still a Malay," Smith replied, without looking at him. He added: "Blood's thicker than water."

"Bushwah!" Hodges looked annoyed.

Hawker leaned forward on his elbows and they grew quiet, waiting for him to speak. He studied Stark, taking his time.

"You've got a point," he said finally.

"What point?" Hodges demanded.

"We can't take any chances," Hawker snapped. "You know damned well the Malays are getting restless. Personally I hadn't thought of that, but I'm thinking of it now."

"It's the war," Hodges defended.

"Sure it's the war, but they got a stake in it, too, and maybe that stake doesn't agree with ours." Stark eyed the superintendent with new respect, thinking the man was deeper than he'd given him credit for. Hawker straightened up as if reaching a decision and stared at his assistant. Hodges glared back.

"Arrange it," Hawker barked suddenly. "Use Smith, Holden, whoever you need. I want that plant covered from here on out—twenty-four hours a day. That'll be your baby." He added malevolently: "That'll give you something to do."

Hodges flushed and looked meanly at Stark. Hawker started to add something when a disturbance came from the porch. Stark and Texas Smith glanced out the window. Gurko Singh, planted in front of the door, was barring the way to a Malay.

"Talo," Smith said briefly.

"More trouble," Hawker groaned. "Call him in."

Smith shouted without moving and the *mandur* of natives entered, halting respectfully just inside the door. Taller than most of his race, he had the slender Malay

50

build, with smooth, unblemished skin and an ageless face. Stark thought he could have been twenty or forty. He wore a wicked-looking parang at his waist—his badge of office. His eyes were inscrutable, his bland features unbroken by any expression whatever.

"What is it?" Hawker growled.

"Trouble, tuan."

"Sure, it's always trouble. What kind of trouble?"

"The sickness, tuan. Four dead."

"Where?" It took Stark an instant to realize the exclamation had come from the company physician. Ebell half-rose from his chair and the *mandur* switched his eyes.

"The powerhouse barracks, tuan."

Hawker swore and looked at the doctor. Ebell pushed back his chair, saying, "I'd better get over there—find out what it is."

"Christ, a plague . . . all we need," Hawker growled. He got noisily to his feet. "I'll go with you."

"Mind if I go along?" Stark asked.

Hawker looked a bit surprised. "Not if you don't mind the risk," he assented. "Some of this stuff can be the death of you." He smiled mirthlessly.

"Don't mind a bit," Stark replied. He saw the approving look in Ebell's face.

The superintendent swung toward Talo. "Get the pickup. The Doc will want to move some bodies," he growled.

"Yes, tuan."

"I'll get my bag," Ebell said, slipping through the door and retreating toward the infirmary.

Stark watched him go, thinking he looked solitary and alone. When they were ready, he and Ebell crawled in back of the truck and sat on a wooden bench built along one side. Hawker climbed in next to Talo, who was driving. The engine roared to life and the vehicle began bouncing over the rough road.

Several small utility buildings flashed by before they crossed a field covered with huge steel tanks, each encompassed by an earthen fire wall. Stark remembered

51

they were passing over a mined area and grimaced. Also, the jolting caused his arm to throb. Ebell remained silent, staring out the side, his face worried.

Coming to a swampy area, Talo shoved the truck into low gear but once or twice the wheels spun before they managed to take hold. Across a rutted clearing the powerhouse came into view and a hundred yards behind it Stark saw the long thatch-roofed barracks building that was their destination. A couple of Malays saw them coming and scurried from sight as Talo swung around to the front of the barracks and stopped. Hawker alighted as Ebell leaped from the truck and hurried toward the entrance.

Stark started to follow but Hawker cautioned, "Better stick around until we know what it is."

He nodded and lit a cigarette, feeling the sweat roll down his face. The sun, glaring and hot, had climbed high in the east. The distant beat of a tom-tom filled the air, and he smelled the tang of gasoline. To one side the tall, fractionating columns of a four-level cracking plant sent wisps of steam into the air, white against the blue of the sky.

After a few minutes Ebell came out, his face wrathful, and walked around to the rear of the building with a stiff, disjointed gait. Stark waited curiously. A short time later the doctor reappeared, his face livid with anger as he glared at Hawker.

"Dysentery," he barked. "Why weren't the latrines built like I ordered?"

"I gave Hodges orders," Hawker snapped defensively.

"Orders! Good God, man, if this thing gets out of hand . . ."

"What do you need?" Hawker quickly cut in.

The tables had not so subtly turned and for the moment the medical officer held command. And for good reason, Stark thought. The disease was the Malays' deadly enemy. Yet he didn't entirely understand Ebell's attitude until the latter snapped: "Those dead men are naked— they've been stripped. Clothes, blankets—everything has

52

been stolen. I want everything back—burned. I want every damned blanket in the place burned. Now," he stated emphatically. Hawker cursed luridly.

Ebell started to turn away, then added: "There are half a dozen more in there sick—in a bad way. We might have an epidemic on our hands."

"Epidemic—Goddamn Hodges," Hawker snarled. His face became mottled with rage.

"Get the others lined up—I want to check them," Ebell cut in.

The superintendent swung toward Talo, roared an order and the latter raced across the clearing to the powerhouse. Within seconds a line of Malays scrambled out, casting backward glances as they crossed the field as if the devil himself followed them. They fell into a ragged line facing the medical officer. Stark noticed they could display fear toward the *mandur*, one of their kind, but the faces they presented toward the others remained impassive.

Talo glanced down the formation, then dashed into the barracks. Shortly afterward another Malay appeared with the *mandur* at his heels, kicking him onward and cursing in a shrill tongue. The native staggered toward his fellow men, seeming to move in a dream as if unaware of his pursuer's brutality. Stark flinched and glanced at Ebell. The latter's face was prim, disapproving.

"Leave it to Talo to pick up the malingerers," Hawker exclaimed with satisfaction.

Ebell didn't bother to reply. When the formation was complete, he started down the line studying each man briefly. He stopped to ask questions several times. He had nearly reached the blank-eyed Malay the *mandur* had driven from the barracks when the man sprang like a tiger, and in a fraction of a second had snatched the parang from Talo's waist. The latter leaped back as if shot. Steel slashed through the air, splitting the skull of a man next to the doctor. The killer spun, whirling the blade, and within seconds two more Malays had died.

"Amok! Amok!" The terrible cry rent the air and the natives scattered in all directions. "Amok! Amok!"

"La illah il Allah," a Malay screamed.

Stark saw the crazed man spin toward the doctor, who stood as if paralyzed. His eyes held a stricken look.

"Watch it," he yelled, at the same time throwing himself forward. He caught a glimpse of the parang swinging down and tried to block it. *Wham! Wham!* The Malay staggered backward, tottering, then let the blade fall gently and slumped to the ground.

Stark swung around. Hawker held a revolver; a thin trickle of blue smoke curled upward from the muzzle.

"Lord, oh, Lord." Ebell suddenly came to life and looking down at the dead man, wiped the sweat from his face. Hawker slipped the weapon back into his pocket.

"Bury the dog," he snarled at Talo. He glanced at Ebell and back again. "Bury 'em all, and I mean bury 'em. Don't throw 'em in the river."

"Yes, Tuan."

"I want to see a fire around here—a damned big fire." His voice quavered with anger.

"Count the blankets," Ebell said mildly. "I want to make sure we get them all."

"Now, by God, I'm going back and chew out Hodges," Hawker gritted. He turned toward the truck without looking back.

Stark lay for a while smoking and rehashing the day's events. Following two more deaths among the Malays, Ebell had transformed the barracks into a field hospital, leaving Yoshi to care for the main infirmary. Suzanne had pitched in to help. The dead had been buried, blankets and clothing burned, the walls and floors scrubbed with strong disinfectants and new stores issued from company supplies.

Now the doctor was working around the clock, hoping to stave off a possible full-scale epidemic. Stark shuddered at contemplation of the deaths of the three Malays under the blade of the native who had run amok, then pushed the unpleasant thought aside in favor of Suzanne.

54

Out of nowhere, or so it seemed, the tall brunette American girl had come striding into his life. Somehow he had known it to be inevitable from the first, and wondered at his surprise. He savored the memory, thinking she was like none he'd ever known before. The thought that this was just the beginning lay delicious in his mind.

A shadow moved beyond the bamboo shades as Gurko Singh rolled in his blanket to sleep on the veranda; the thought that the giant Bengali had become his self-appointed bodyguard brought a smile to his lips. Quashing out the cigarette, he was preparing for sleep when he detected stealthy movement followed by a light tapping at his door.

"Joe . . ." He recognized Selinda Hawker's voice and became instantly alert. Emergency? He was about to tell her to wait when the call came again. Answering, he pulled the single blanket over his naked body as she entered, standing like a shadow just inside the room.

"Anything wrong?" he asked tersely.

"I . . . don't know." He felt a brief alarm until she added: "There's something I have to tell you."

"Here . . . now?" He struggled with his thoughts, wondering what to expect.

"I know it's late," she quickly stated, "but Mike's away in the field."

"Oh . . ." He remembered the brief byplay at the party and let the amusement creep into his voice. So Selinda . . .

"It's about the question you asked," she quickly said, as if sensing his reaction.

"About Saito?" he asked sharply.

"Yes, about that, too."

"What about Saito?" He tried to keep the excitement from his voice.

"May I sit down?"

"Yes, certainly."

He watched her move to the side of the bed and sit on the edge, drawing her white gown closer around her. The movement seemed sensual, deliberate, and he didn't speak, deciding to let her take the initiative. She eyed him steadily before speaking.

"I know who you are." The statement came so suddenly that he was taken aback. What did she know, and how much? Or was she just fishing?

He answered quietly, "Of course, you know. I'm Joe Stark, age thirty-two, six-foot and dark hair . . ." In the pale light he saw her wan smile and stopped, thinking it was no good. She did know. "Go ahead," he added.

"Joe Stark, Naval Intelligence," she stated quietly.

"Okay, so we'll start from there. What makes you think that?"

She hesitated, and when she spoke her voice was toneless as if reciting some litany. "After Driscoll was killed, Mike told me who he really was. I guess he wasn't expecting anyone else to come. Then when you asked the same questions—well, I knew." She stopped, watching his face.

He said carefully, "Assuming you're right, why are you here now?"

"I've been thinking about it, about your questions."

"About Saito?"

"Yes, that and other things. Now, with what's happening, I can't keep quiet any longer. I have to tell you what I know." He relaxed back against the bed. Maybe this was what he'd been waiting for. The break. He quietly asked, "Then you know about Saito?"

"Yes."

"From where?" he prodded.

"From Obak . . . and others."

"Who is Saito?" he challenged.

"I don't know that," she aswered firmly.

He decided her voice rang true, and continued. "What have you heard?"

"Well, just rumors."

"Just rumors?" he mocked. She raised her head defiantly.

"I hear things, partly because . . ." She finished speaking, running her tongue nervously over her lips.

"Because you're Malay?" he asked bluntly.

"Yes, of course." She raised her head proudly. "My grandfather came from Holland."

So that accounted for her European mannerisms, he thought. The silence built up and abruptly he asked, "What specifically have you heard about Saito?"

"Only the name."

"And nothing else?"

She stared at him and said tonelessly: "Yoshi—somehow they're connected."

"Yoshi?" He failed to conceal his surprise. "What about her?"

"I don't know. That's why I didn't say anything before. Supposing I'm wrong? It's just gossip—something Obak picked up. He says she goes to Telukta every Friday night and somehow there's a connection. I really don't know."

"Where's Telukta?"

"A small settlement down the road—on the outskirts of Palembang," she said.

His questioning elicited the information that it had a small, good district inhabited by many of the Palembang merchants; the rest of the area contained mainly Malays and Indians. She didn't know anyone from there personally.

He asked, "But you don't know why she goes?"

"No, I told you that."

"Why are you telling me all this now?"

"Because . . . there's something more." She glanced away and then brought her eyes back again, probing and weighing as if uncertain how much to confide.

"Well . . ." He waited.

Finally she continued: "Obak says Tombuk has been bragging about going into the tiger field at night."

"Oh . . ." He assimilated the information, recalling the native had been used to fill in as a houseboy on the night of the party. "Doesn't he work at the infirmary?"

"With Yoshi," she said.

"Have you told your husband this?"

57

"Mike? No."

"Why not?"

She studiously rocked on the edge of the bed staring at the wall, and finally said, "Because he's in love with her."

"Your husband . . . with Yoshi?" he exclaimed. Somehow the thought seemed preposterous—the burly Hawker and Ebell's slim nurse.

She watched him steadily. "You find that strange?"

"Yes, frankly I do," he admitted.

"You shouldn't. This place does strange things, and Mike's no saint. Before her it was Martha Hodges." She caught his expression and added: "Oh, I know, you can't see how these things could happen. You ought to live here a few years," she ended bitterly.

"But your husband hasn't any suspicions about Yoshi?" he probed.

She said tiredly, "Probably not."

"How do you feel about . . . everything?"

"About Mike?" He nodded and she tossed her head disdainfully. "A wife has to look the other way."

He hesitated to use the word "native," then finally asked, "Which of the boys can be trusted?"

"Talo," she declared without hesitation.

"How about Obak?"

"Well, he too."

"Why the sudden decision to tell all this?" he asked curiously.

"Because of the planes, and everything that's happening. Don't you see, Joe, I'm scared." She leaned forward and he saw that above the waist, at least, she wore nothing under her gown. Her breasts caught the pale light, small and daintily curved, and he felt an instant reaction. "I feel as if I were alone with the whole world caving in—"

"It's not that bad," he cut in, trying to keep the tremor from his voice. Hawker's wife was a desirable woman.

She stifled a sob. "I don't wont to be alone, Joe."

He felt a small urging, a pooling of his body blood and memory of Suzanne stirred in his mind, bringing a quick

58

stab of guilt. He said resolutely, "I don't know what help I can be." The words sounded inane in his ears.

"I don't know. All I know is that I need you," she whispered. Her voice held a passionate quality that didn't escape him.

"You'll think differently later," he replied, without conviction.

"When Mike returns?" she asked edgily. "Don't you understand what I've been trying to tell you? I hate him, hate everything about this place. Do you know what it's like? Endless days, endless nights, nothing but talk of oil. A woman grows old here, old before her time and has nothing—no life, no love." She leaned forward, placing her hand on his bare shoulder. It felt hot and cold at the same time and despite himself he stared at her breasts for a moment before tearing his eyes away.

"He's your husband, Selinda." He flushed at the thought of his hypocrisy.

"Husband!" She uttered the word with asperity. "Husband to Martha Hodges, to Yoshi Kusaka and God knows who else."

"I think you're wrong, at least about Martha Hodges," he stated, remembering how Hawker had castigated the woman.

She tossed her head disdainfully. "Why, because of how he acts toward her now?"

He nodded.

"He grows tired of a woman, Joe. He's got to have someone new, someone different all the time. Don't you think I know how he sneaks to Yoshi at nights? Not that I mind." She tossed her head in defiance. "I have my own life to live."

"Yoshi doesn't look like the type," he observed.

"What can you tell about how a woman thinks, Joe? No one knows that but a woman." Her voice became toneless again. "It's like my being here now, offering myself because I need you, but the world can't see that."

"Listen, please . . ."

59

"Joe . . ." She leaned farther forward and her small breasts pressed against him, her lips brushed his cheek. Involuntarily he closed his hands around her waist, kneading the firm, vibrant flesh. She whimpered and began whispering passionately into his ear. For a moment he surrendered, then desire fought with conscience and conscience won.

Reluctantly he pushed her away, saying, "I'm a guest in Mike's house, Selinda."

"That doesn't matter," she said brokenly.

"It does to me."

"Why, because of the American girl?" Even in the dim light he saw the mute look in her eyes.

"No, not exactly," he lied. He brooded a moment. "You'd better go."

"All right." She stared at him, edging her lips with her tongue and he felt an ungovernable desire. "Kiss me—kiss me once," she demanded.

"Selinda . . ."

She pressed her lips to his mouth, silencing him, and her tongue touched his lips, darting. For an instant he felt a wave of guilt; it became mingled with a surge of desire until nothing remained but the slim, fiery woman kissing him. She moved her lips to his ear, promising passion, endearments, everything. Her words said she was hungry, lonely, needed him; her hands caressed him. He felt his resolve tumble, crash under her fierce surrender. Her body was alive with a thousand movements.

He pushed her away and kicked back the cover, and she rose, flinging off the white gown. She had a small body, slim, with breasts like pears, flat of belly with rounded hips. Her lips were parted—he could see her small breasts rise and fall with her rapid breathing. She flung herself toward him with fire and he forgot his earlier misgivings, forgot everything except this woman in his arms. She was Aspara, Anna Sing Kai—every woman he'd ever known rolled into one.

"Joe, Joe . . ." she moaned. A tidal wave rolled over

them, the world seemed to vanish. He heard only her fierce whisperings.

The night was far gone before she left. He heard her sandals patter across the hardwood floor. Afterwards there was silence.

✿ seven

STARK AWOKE to the howling of a troop of monkeys and the deep thud of a tom-tom calling the native workers to a new day. The events of the preceding night flashed through his mind and he reached for his cigarettes, feeling guilty, then lit one and blew a cloud of smoke toward the ceiling.

The measured beat of the great hollow tree drum vividly recalled the primitive nature of this land into which Durling had sent him. Despite the huge oil refineries and the coffee and rubber plantations which checkerboarded the lowland jungles of the east coast, the island had all the aspects of a lost world—a land of steep-pitched volcanic mountains, swampy jungles, of bats, boars, tree-shrews and flying foxes; a crazy, deadly land where odd-helmeted hornbills, looking like buffoons, and lemurs with tragicomic eyes stared from murky depths inhabited by monstrous animals and slim brown men who moved furtively and killed with deadly blowguns.

It was also a land where human passions ran wild, where the blood flowed hot and the towers of inhibition quickly tumbled. Bad enough in normal times, it now had taken on the added dimensions of war, pestilence, murder. Durling, he thought grimly, had tossed him a curve.

He had deliberately tried to keep his mind off Selinda but she crept back into his thoughts; he felt guilty and

61

excited at the same time. She was dynamite. The super-intendent's beautiful Oriental wife had proved to be a sex bomb.

Was she so different from other women he'd known? He mused over the question. The difference seemed to be in degrees of passion, not in willingness. The wife of an insurance executive in San Diego, the daughter of a banker in Washington, a well-known society woman in Honolulu . . . they approached the barrier in different ways, but all had crossed it. Willingly. No, it wasn't the tropics at all, he decided. It was something else. Maybe he traveled a magic path.

He shifted his thoughts to Selinda, deliberately brushing aside the memory of her slim body while he tried to recall her exact words and intonations, wondering how much to believe or disbelieve.

An affair between Hawker and the still attractive, gray-ing Martha Hodges was quite likely, but he couldn't recon-cile the burly superintendent with the dainty Japanese nurse. Such an affair sounded as incongruous as the mating of a bull and a fawn. Not that Hawker wasn't willing; he knew that from his earlier observations concerning Suzanne Ebell. But he couldn't see Yoshi as willing.

More important, why had Selinda so suddenly decided to talk? He wasn't sure, but suspected the affair of the previous night had been well planned. She had entered wearing only the white wrap, sure of herself; sure of him. And the night had taught him she was no green hand.

Like Aspara, she knew every subtle way of intoxicating a man—his pulse quickened at the memory. He would guess the story about Hawker and Yoshi to be pure fabri-cation to arouse his sympathy or serve as an excuse for Selinda's own derelictions were it not for one fact—she knew his identity. He couldn't dismiss that, just as he couldn't dismiss the possibility that Yoshi was something more than she appeared. Were the visits to Telukta fig-ments of Selinda's imagination, or did they occur, and if so, why? He'd have to explore that.

Whatever the mystery of Saito, Driscoll's death, and

the attempt on his own life, one thing lay certain in his mind—both women somehow were involved. Selinda knew too much. And Yoshi? Both Hawker and Ebell had defended the girl, yet how much did either know about her? Little, he suspected. In the welter of cross-currents in which he had become involved, one steady signal rang in his mind: he could trust no one. How would he make it up to Suzanne? Well, that was another secret he'd have to push deep into his subconscious. One of many.

By the time he had shaved and dressed, Obak had his breakfast ready; almost, Stark thought, as if he had been waiting behind the door for the first sound of movement.

The houseboy's furtiveness disturbed him, and wryly he wondered if perhaps the man had listened during Selinda's night visit. While he ate, he covertly studied Obak's impassive face, thinking he well could be the key to the baffling complex of problems facing him. His body build and features marked him as a Batak from the wild mountains above Lake Toba.

Divided almost equally among Moslems, Christians and heathens, he remembered them as a patriarchal race which built weird, horned-roof houses on stilts, had communal halls, were proficient in rice-farming, weaving, pottery—the use of the deadly blowgun. Tombuk, too, was a Batak. He refrained from questions, sensing he would get but a bland smile in return; doubtless the Malay would pretend not to understand.

Hawker had returned sometime during the early hours of the dawn and now his mud-spattered pickup truck stood just outside the door. Stark contemplated it briefly, finished eating and went into the garden to smoke. The heat had come almost instantly with the sun, which now, smoky-red, rested just above the horizon. He felt a slight breeze, the slow, steady push of the moisture-laden northeast monsoon which blew from September to March and occasionally erupted into wild storms known as *sumatras*.

While debating how to pursue the rumor about Tombuk, he saw Hawker emerge from the house, stopping on the veranda to light his pipe. Stark thought he was seeing

63

the man through new eyes. At the moment he appeared something more than merely the ruffian boss of a jungle oil empire, but he saw nothing hidden in the man's blunt speech and manner. Lover of Martha Hodges? Yoshi? Perhaps. But one thing he knew beyond doubt; Hawker also was husband to a wantonly passionate stack of dynamite clothed in an utterly lovely and abandoned body.

The superintendent walked down to join him and he murmured a good morning. Hawker returned the greeting with a nod, staring somberly over the compound. In the morning light his face looked tired and, Stark thought, a trifle wistful. He couldn't have had more than a few hours of sleep. The jagged scar across his cheek was etched whitely against the stubble of his dark beard, and he felt a quick sympathy; Hawker had problems.

After a decent interval of silence, he asked, "How's the sick list coming?"

Hawker blew a cloud of smoke before answering. "Not so good. We lost a couple more last night and have another half a dozen down—the Doc's afraid of a full-scale epidemic." His eyes brooded. "That could be damned tough, especially now that we need every hand we can muster. Smith, Holden and Hodges are trading off on the powerhouse watch but that leaves me pretty short in the field."

"If I can help," he suggested.

"You might at that," Hawker agreed. "Know anything about setting up ignition systems?"

"A little."

"We might need you there. I'll let you know if we do."

They discussed the situation for a while. Hawker was of the opinion the Japanese attack could come any day, any hour, and had prepared for the rumble downstream which would mark the beginning of destruction of the Royal Dutch and other Plaju River refineries. "After that we'll only have hours," he concluded.

"But you're prepared?"

"As prepared as we'll ever be," he admitted, staring gloomily toward the distant oil reservoirs. "Sometimes I

64

think I'll be glad to see it happen—getting the waiting over. Hodges was right on that score—the attack is a cinch."

"But you've still got to wait."

"Yeah, we have to wait. If by some miracle . . ." He didn't finish. Stark nodded sympathetically. After a while Hawker stirred.

"Twelve years," he mused. "It's a damned big chunk of my life. At times I wonder if it is worth it."

"You won't be starting over," Stark said.

"No, the company will send me somewhere—another spot, another hellhole. This goddamned oil always seems to be at the ends of the earth.

"But you like it?"

"Hell, yes, I like it. That's the damnable part. Anybody could build a field on the outskirts of Tulsa."

"You've done a tremendous job."

"Sure, I know that. That's why I'm so damned proud of the place, but it isn't right that I should destroy it. I'm a builder, not a wrecker. They should send someone else for that." His anger revealed his deep emotion and Stark felt he knew what Hawker was going through. The huge oil field with its vast refineries and tanks had become an integral part of him. He suspected that Hodges regarded the plant as merely a means of salary, or perhaps for the power his position gave, while to Hawker the black oil sucked up from beneath the jungles constituted the blood of his veins. The superintendent stirred, settling his eyes on the truck.

"Well, I'd better be getting along . . . see how things are coming."

"I'll be out after I get my arm dressed," he offered. Hawker nodded, tapped the ashes from his pipe and strode to the truck. Stark watched it bounce down the rutted road before turning toward the infirmary. Yoshi, bandaging a Malay's wounded hand, didn't look up at his entrance. When she finished with the native, he asked, "Is Doctor Ebell in?"

"No, he's at the field hospital." Her eyes weighed him

65

without expression, and he returned the stare, trying to picture her in the role of lover—spy. Neither picture quite came off.

"Thought I'd get the bandage changed early, if you don't mind."

"Not at all," she replied crisply.

She came over and fingered the dressing; suddenly jerked the tape loose, apparently not noticing his grimace. Cleaning the wounds, she inspected them, then removed the stitches and swabbed the area with disinfectant.

He watched her replace the bandage, thinking she didn't appear to fit the role in which Selinda had cast her. Dainty, almost fragile features and a white comb in her black hair gave her a doll-like aspect, but her body beneath the white uniform suggested that of a lovely woman, if he were to judge by the full contours and rhythmic movement as she worked. He quite easily could see Hawker going overboard, or almost anyone else for that matter.

The last bandage in place, she said gravely, "There, now if you'll come tomorrow . . ."

Their eyes met and locked and he hesitated briefly before saying, "Thank you, I will."

She nodded without answering and he left, walking out under a polished sky. Martha Hodges waved from the veranda of the small house she occupied with her husband and he automatically turned his steps in that direction. Smiling crisply, she looked down at him from the top of the stairs and asked, "How is the arm?"

"Good as new," he assured her, halting at the bottom step. She wore a blue housecoat over what he assumed was her nightgown and pin curlers held her graying hair, but despite those drawbacks she possessed an attractiveness that belied her years. Her unlined face and figure were more than passable. She caught his scrutiny.

"You'll have to excuse me. I never dress before noon— a habit in the islands," she added. "Care for coffee, American-style?"

"Nothing I'd like better," he answered, thinking of the horrible brew Obak made.

"Cream or sugar?"

"Black . . . and strong," he added. "I need it."

She laughed. "Sit down. I'll bring it." Motioning toward a table on the veranda, she vanished into the house. He heard her stirring around inside. Returning with two cups, she placed one before him and sat in a long chair next to the table juggling hers and smiling musingly.

"Not many men tangle with a tiger and live to tell about it." Cool, gray eyes searched him.

"Just lucky," he answered with a nonchalant shrug.

"How did it happen?" She caught his hesitancy and added, "Don't mind me. I'm curious. I've been trying to figure whatever in the world you were doing in the tiger field, especially at night."

"A newcomer," he admitted, "just taking a walk." He fingered his cup, hearing her low, delightful laugh, but he saw no doubt in her face.

"That's one way of getting excitement," she concluded.

"I don't recommend it."

"No, but you've got to admit, it's novel."

They laughed, then talked for a while about the islands and the States. Like Hawker, both she and her husband had been raised in Tulsa. His first job had been in the oil fields, twenty years with this same company. Married sixteen year and no children, she spoke of their barrenness with a note of wistfulness. Finally the conversation began to trail off.

"Jasper working?" he asked politely.

"Night and day. Personally, I'll be glad when it comes to an end—eight years are too long. It will be good to get home again, see some lights and paved streets and talk with old friends." She laughed suddenly and, he thought, a bit bitterly. "They think I'm lucky being out here—that the island is some sort of paradise. . . ."

She broke off talking and he wondered if her husband understood her resentment. Certainly eight years in Palembang was a long time, for man or woman. She set her cup on the edge of the table.

67

"Maybe we can start over again." Her eyes studied the distance.

"Of course, you can," he assured her.

"Maybe, I don't know." She glanced at him. "We're not the same people we were once; this place does things to one. Our values change—become twisted, I guess."

He saw the regret in her face.

"It's a rough country," he agreed.

"Especially for a woman, Mr. Stark."

"Call me Joe."

"And I'm Martha." She glanced away again and the silence built up. Finally she murmured, "I honestly don't know if I want to start over—maybe it's too late."

"It's never too late," he stated.

"No? This place is different for a woman. A man has his job, something to keep him going, but for a woman there's nothing; not even the pleasure of planting a garden or keeping house. We have boys for that. There's nothing—just heat and mosquitoes and malaria. After a while you start grasping, reaching for a bit of life; then you no longer care. It's like skiing downhill—you go faster and faster.

"You can put on the brakes," he suggested tacitly.

"That's just it, you don't want brakes. You want . . . everything." She looked away quickly.

Stark knew she was talking about herself, revealing the very things with which Hawker had branded her, and momentarily he felt discomfited, thinking he didn't want to become a father confessor. Yet, at the moment, he felt he completely understood her. Perhaps if her husband had been a different kind of person . . . She laughed, a trilling laugh, breaking the spell. She brought her face back into a composed smile.

"Don't mind me. It's good to talk to someone occasionally. It's so seldom I get the chance that I go overboard when I do."

He nodded. "I don't mind in the least."

"I think I got to feeling sorry for myself, with this war

and everything. I started and couldn't stop, but I promise not to do it again."

He started to reply when the edge of his eye caught sight of Hawker's truck bouncing back along the rutted road and he turned to watch it, sensing trouble.

"Trouble?" she asked quietly.

"No, I don't think so," he lied. "I told Hawker I'd help him in the field today. He's probably coming to get me." He set down the cup. "Thanks for the American-style coffee, Mrs. Hodges. I appreciate it after Obak's brew."

"Martha," she corrected. Her eyes lingered on his face as she added: "I make it every morning."

"I'll remember that." He got up and started down the stairs, then heard her call softly and paused to look back.

"Take care of yourself," she urged.

"Sure," he promised. She smiled wistfully and he continued toward the main house, reaching it just as the superintendent leaped from the truck. His flushed, sweaty face wore an angry scowl.

"Trouble?" Stark asked.

"Nothing but." Hawker faced him. "The damned coolies are taking off on us."

"Deserting?"

"Like rats. About half of them just melted into the jungles and Lord knows when the rest will follow. I told Talo to hold them if he had to kill them to do it."

"The epidemic?" Stark asked.

Hawker threw up his hands in a gesture of defeat. "Hell, no, we've ridden through those before. This is something else—something I don't like."

"What?" he demanded.

"Damned if I know but I'm going to find out."

Stark experienced a sinking sensation. "How will this affect the demolition program?"

"It sure as hell won't help," Hawker snapped. "We can get most of it, thanks to the way we have it set up, but there's still a lot of machinery to be smashed—odds and ends. It might take more time than we have."

69

Stark said bluntly, "You've got to get everything."

"Sure, I know." Hawker stared toward the office. "I'll give Vandervoort a call, see what's happening down there." He turned away and strode into the office, slamming the door behind him.

Fretting, Stark waited, trying to assess the worst that could happen. Hawker had a score of drillers covering the long jungle pipeline, so it could be blown up even if all the Malays deserted. On the other hand, the coolie gangs were needed to plug the well bores, but that was far less important than the refinery itself.

After a while Hawker emerged with an angry scowl, exclaiming, "Vandervoort's lost a few but nowhere near what we have. He says they caught a Malay trying to get the others to desert."

"Oh?" The pattern formed in Stark's mind.

"I understand they shot him," he stated with satisfaction.

"Saito," Stark said musingly. He looked at the oil superintendent. "He's come into the light."

"Who?" Hawker looked puzzled.

"Saito, the man I was asking about. He's trying to deliver the field to the Japs intact," he explained.

A look of comprehension crossed Hawker's face. "So that's it."

"That's it," Stark affirmed grimly.

"Then we've got one of those birds around here."

"Looks that way," he assented.

"By God, if I catch the man . . ."

"Tombuk?" Stark interjected quietly.

"Tombuk?" Hawker brought his head up with a startled look, and he demanded: "What gave you that idea?"

"A hunch," he lied.

The superintendent laughed mirthlessly. "You can't pin it on him."

"No?"

"No—he was killed this morning."

"Killed?" It was Stark's turn to be startled.

"Dead as a doorknob," Hawker stated. "Someone got

70

him with a blowgun." Stark didn't reply immediately, trying to fit the pieces together. If Selinda were right, Tombuk looked like the man who had lured him into the tiger field. Now he was dead. To shut his mouth? Undoubtedly that was it. The Malay had been a tool—Saito's tool; but he had talked too much. Saito, he thought, must be very close.

Hawker asked abruptly, "What did you have in mind?"

"Nothing, nothing really."

Hawker gazed over the compound and Stark saw he already had dismissed the subject. The superintendent brought his attention back.

"I'd better get along. I'll send Hodges in to take over the office in case something comes up. If you don't mind sticking around . . ."

"Not a bit," Stark assured him.

He watched the truck disappear across the field before glancing toward the office. Selinda Hawker stood on the veranda appearing very cool. Slowly she descended the steps and strolled toward him.

"Good morning, Joe."

"Good morning," he answered gruffly, feeling a slight annoyance whose roots he realized were founded in guilt.

"My, you sound cross." Her voice was teasing but there was nothing teasing about her dark eyes. Smoldering, dancing with little flames, they searched his face.

"I'm not," he denied.

"He's gone." She glanced meaningfully down the road along which the truck had disappeared.

He sucked his lip, then swung toward her.

"Look, last night just happened, but it can't happen again. It's over and gone."

"No," she said calmly.

"It's got to be that way."

"Because I'm married?"

"That's it," he said shortly.

"Joe, are you trying to tell me that I'm the first married woman you ever made love to?" He saw the amusement in her face and flushed.

71

"I'm not proud of it," he admitted.

"Neither am I." Unexpectedly she reached out and touched his arm. "Don't you think I have feelings, too? But we're driven—do what we have to do. Do you think I could have remained alone in my room with you down there? I'm a woman, Joe, and there have been too many lonely nights. Who's to be our judge?"

"I judge myself. I have a conscience," he said stonily, thinking of Suzanne.

"Do women often throw themselves at your feet?" she mocked. When he didn't reply, her face changed, becoming intent. "I'd do anything—"

"You already have."

"And I will again." Her voice fell, becoming low and toneless. "Could any woman do more?"

"No," he admitted.

"Don't you see, there is no path back."

"There is for me."

"No, Joe. Last night wouldn't have happened if you hadn't needed me as much as I did you." Her eyes beseeched him and momentarily he felt caught between powerful opposing forces.

He brushed the intimacies of the night from his mind, saying, "I've got to go. I have work to do."

"All right." Lightly she touched his arm again, then walked toward the veranda. Halfway up the stairs she stopped and looked back.

"Tonight, Joe Stark."

She was gone before he could answer.

✿ eight

STARK FACED the day with growing impatience, fretting over his promise to remain near the office until Hodges returned. The episode with Selinda marred his thoughts of Suzanne, and he cursed himself for a fool.

When he considered the hour appropriate, he walked to Ebell's cottage and knocked at the door several times before he realized there was no one home. Disappointed, he went to the dispensary and questioned Yoshi, learning that Suzanne had gone to the field hospital with her father.

She's dodging me, he thought; she feels guilty. She wasn't one to enter lightly into an affair. He felt a pang of conscience, aware of Yoshi watching him. She was between patients and he took advantage of it to start a running conversation, hoping to draw her out. She parried his questions deftly and finally, frustrated at being able to accomplish nothing more than aimless chatter, he left, but not before he saw a touch of amusement crinkle her lips. The Japanese girl made him feel gauche. Martha Hodges rescued him with another cup of coffee and they chatted until he saw a car coming from the powerhouse.

"Jasper," she said. He didn't answer. Hodges pulled to a stop in front of the house and jumped out, his face a sour scowl.

"Everything all right?" Martha called. He didn't answer until he reached the steps, then glanced at them dark-faced.

"All right, hell," he gritted. "Half the coolies have taken to the hills and Hawker's ranting like a madman."

"The coolies . . . gone?" she asked, startled.

"Gone, and if we were smart, we'd be gone, too. We won't have a chance in hell if we stick around much longer."

73

"We have an escape route." she declared firmly. He didn't answer.

Stark caught a whiff of alcohol and realized Hodges had been drinking; Martha must have sensed it for she exchanged a swift look with him.

"Any calls from Vandervoort?" Hodges demanded, glaring at Stark.

"Nothing since Hawker called earlier," he answered complacently. Hodges grunted and stomped into the house, slamming the door behind him.

Martha asked quietly, "What does it mean, the Malays leaving?"

"I don't know," Stark answered truthfully. "We might have a bit more trouble destroying the plant but it certainly doesn't affect Hawker's escape plans."

He didn't know whether it did or not but the relief in her face made him glad for the lie. He found himself liking her; she was a good sort, he thought. Just unlucky—a victim of Sumatra. Lord, anyone would break after eight years. Murmuring something, he left, wishing Suzanne would return.

By noon Hodges was drunk—roaring, profanely drunk. He had taken a bottle to Hawker's office, drunk steadily, and when he had emptied it, swore until Obak brought more. Realizing the man's ugly mood and fearing trouble, Stark remained in the vicinity.

Later Hodges stumbled from the office, cursing luridly at Gurko Singh, who sat on the steps. The Bengali arose and moved aside, his face impassive. Hodges staggered down the stairs toward Stark.

"By God, if I'm going to wait any longer," he roared, "Hawker can have this place. I'm getting out."

Stark flipped his cigarette away. "Take it easy," he counseled.

"Take it easy," Hodges sneered. He swayed slightly, watching Stark with bloodshot eyes.

"Anything wrong with that?" Stark asked.

"How the hell can you take it easy? Boy, you don't

know the score around here." Hodges attempted to pull himself erect.

"And you do?"

"I know plenty," he mumbled.

"You're unnecessarily worried," Stark stated, with a confidence he didn't feel. "Everything will be all right."

"Sure, everything will be all right. We'll wind up dead. You, too, Dead—like Driscoll."

Stark became suddenly alert. "What about Driscoll?"

"He's dead, that's what."

"Sure, I know that," he replied, wondering what the other was driving at. Hodges' eyes grew cagey.

"Think you know all the answers, don't you?" he sneered. "You big handsome bastards and Selinda—"

"What was that?" Stark cut in, startled.

"Selinda—Driscoll was making out." He stopped speaking, swaying, and his eyes began to glaze over. "I know what's going on. . . ."

He would have fallen if Stark hadn't caught him. Looking around, he saw Selinda watching from the veranda; her face mocked him. Cursing, he put Hodges' arm around his neck and half-dragged him to his house, where he found Martha waiting by the door.

"Where to?" Stark tried to keep his tone light.

"The bedroom," she replied, smiling wanly. She nodded toward a door and he carried him inside, depositing him on a bed. Hodges immediately rolled over and began to snore.

"A drink or so too much," Stark observed.

She smiled bitterly. "It's always a drink or so too much. Now maybe you can understand why I am like I am."

"I think you're very nice," he answered, feeling sorry for her.

"Nice! You know better than that. I know what people say." She leaned back against the wall and stared at him. "But I guess they're right. I just can't help it. It's things like this—years of this."

Memory of the passionate kisses she had exchanged with Pete Holden flicked through his mind. Well, she was no

75

worse than Selinda Hawker or, for that matter, any number of other women he had known.

"Take it easy, settle down," he advised. "You're as-good as anyone."

She smiled mockingly. "That wouldn't have to be very good, would it?"

"There aren't many angels," he admitted. "I'd better go—cover the office until he recovers. If you need me . . ." He broke off the words, glancing toward the door.

"By that time it'll be morning," she answered listlessly. "Thank you, Joe."

"Don't mention it."

"You're nice."

"No, I'm no better than anyone else. I have my foibles too."

"I know, but you're still nice—the nicest person that's come along. You'd better go now."

When he left she was standing by the bed gazing down at her husband with an expression that could be either pity or loathing—he didn't know which.

That evening Hawker returned for dinner. He had showered, shaved and changed to a pair of casual tan slacks and gay sport shirt; Stark thought he looked quite presentable. Sitting at the table, the superintendent brushed aside the troubles of the day, merely mentioning that the threatened epidemic appeared under control. There had been no recent deaths and only two or three additional patients. He became expansive as he discussed the preparations for demolishing the plant. Selinda let her husband ramble on without interruption.

Stark found the scene incongruous—the burly Hawker, almost as tall as himself, his dark eyes alive, his florid face gleaming under the light of the copper lamps; Selinda, serene and composed, playing the role of the dutiful wife; Obak, standing in the shadows, wearing a white jacket and an absolutely expressionless face.

He glanced at Hawker's wife, thinking she was a consummate actress. The previous night she had been fire and fury, reckless in her abandonment; now her eyes rested on his face, innocent and without guile, and he thought: *She could fool Hawker forever.* So she had been Driscoll's lover, too? He had no doubt of her true nature—her face and manner masked a soul that plumbed the depths, her last restraint had gone. Well, she could chalk off Joe Stark. That pigeon had flown the coop, he promised himself.

"So Hodges got drunk again?" Hawker was saying. He looked at the ONI man. "That's the trouble with the bastard. You can't trust him. Give him a job to do and he hits the bottle. I should have fired him years ago."

"He was terribly profane," Selinda murmured demurely. "I had to shut my ears." Stark suppressed a laugh. She let her eyes brush his face and lifted her fork. "I feel sorry for poor Martha."

"Poor Martha!" Hawker laughed boisterously. "She's getting hers."

"Hush, that's not nice," she reproved.

"Hell, everyone knows it," he insisted. "Not that I blame her, with a drunk like that."

Stark had a mental image of horns on the superintendent's head and shifted uncomfortably as Selinda commented: "Some people can't help it. They're pushed by circumstances." She glanced at Stark.

"Martha—pushed?" Hawker guffawed. "Hell, she runs 'em down."

"Please," she remonstrated. Her face became intent and she changed the subject. "Are you through for the day?"

"Gotta go out to the field for a few hours, check up on some things," he replied. "I won't be long."

"That's too bad," she murmured sympathetically. She turned her face to Stark and he saw the smoldering look again, her tongue edging her lips. He finished the meal in silence, hoping he was half the actor she was. Later they smoked and chatted. After a decent interval, he excused himself and returned to his room, aware her glance followed him.

77

He waited till the fall of darkness before going outside. A stiff breeze had sprung up and huge black cloud masses rolled across the sky creating shifting gulfs in which the stars gleamed softly. Lighting a cigarette, he smoked while the cool wind brushed his body; its dampness promised rain. He flicked his eyes toward the house; Hawker hadn't left yet.

He walked toward the infirmary, circled it and went to Ebell's cottage. The absence of lights told him Suzanne hadn't returned, and stifling his disappointment, he sat on the porch to smoke. Lamplight filtered through the curtains of Yoshi's house and once or twice he caught her shadowy profile as she passed in front of a window. Yoshi . . .

Wondering about her, he flicked the butt of his cigarette away and lit another, drawing the smoke into his lungs. After a while he heard the roar of Hawker's truck speeding down the powerhouse road, then silence.

Beginning to think Suzanne wouldn't return, he caught movement in the darkness and stiffened, cupping his cigarette and waiting. A figure moved at the edge of the shadows and he grew tense. Hawker! He recognized the man's huge form. So, Hawker had parked the truck. . . .

Silently he cursed the odor of his tobacco, hoping the superintendent wouldn't detect it. Hawker passed within a dozen yards of where he sat and went to Yoshi's door, rapping softly. It opened and for a scant few seconds Stark saw the nurse's slim body silhouetted against the lamplight before Hawker passed into the room.

So Selinda had been right—Hawker and Yoshi were lovers! Utterly incongruous as it seemed, there it was, the small fragile Yoshi and the hulking superintendent. He conjured the relationship in his mind and found it distasteful. He had to admit that Yoshi and Selinda were very much alike, at least physically, and he'd seen nothing alien in the latter's marriage. He puzzled over it before bringing his mind back to more practical things. The relationship between Hawker and the nurse had connotations that disturbed him. If Selinda had been right on that score, chances were she was right on Yoshi's other activities— her mysterious trips to Telukta.

He shifted restlessly. Christ, and Yoshi had a pipeline to Hawker. Doubtless she knew everything that happened, every precaution made to destroy the field. He cursed silently, thinking his job suddenly had doubled in complexity. He couldn't very well confront Hawker with his knowledge, or Yoshi either; by the same token he couldn't afford to let it pass. The lamp in Yoshi's house blinked out. He waited, watching the night, wondering what Durling would do if placed in the same situation. After a while he caught the humor of it and began to hum.

He had started to grow restless again when he heard the sound of an engine and shortly afterward saw headlights reflecting against the infirmary window. A light truck chugged around the corner, stopped and Suzanne hopped out.

"Thank you," she called. The truck moved off and as she came toward him, Stark rose.

"Hello," he said.

She halted, jerking up her head. "You scared me."

"I didn't mean to," he apologized. "I've been waiting, hoping you'd come." She fumbled in her bag without answering, took out a cigarette; he produced a light, holding it while she inhaled. The flame revealed the fatigue in her face.

"You look bushed," he said.

"I am."

"Your father must be, also. He should have come home with you."

"I tried to coax him . . ." She stopped talking and he realized something had disturbed her.

Stepping closer, he asked, "Anything wrong?"

"You shouldn't be here."

"Why?" he asked quietly. She puffed rapidly on the cigarette before answering. "Because . . . I'm a fool."

"You're talking nonsense," he replied gruffly.

"Am I, Joe?" She searched his face. "What must you think of me?"

"I think you're wonderful."

"Yes, and what else must you think?"

"I don't know what you mean," he answered.

She said stonily, "It was so easy for you. You must think it happens all the time—that I'm like some of these other women."

"Listen—" he stepped forward and grasped her by the shoulders—"I don't think any such thing. I think you're sweet and wonderful, and I know exactly what happened. It was spontaneous."

"That's no excuse."

"It's excuse enough for me," he answered. She nervously flicked the ashes from her cigarette, staring him in the face.

"It can't happen again, Joe."

"That's all right, Suzanne. Later, when we leave this damnable island—"

"Neither now nor later," she cut in coldly.

"Not if it's legal?" he asked softly. She stood deathly still, staring at him, and he fancied he could hear the thumping of her heart. "Answer me," he said finally.

She stirred. "Joe . . ."

"I'm proposing."

"Oh, Joe." She moved forward and pushed her face into his shoulder, sobbing. He stroked her head, bewildered, and asked. "What's wrong?"

She looked up. "You fool. You wonderful fool."

"I guess I am. I should have said that before," he admitted. Pulling her closer he kissed her tenderly, seeing the wetness in her eyes. Pushing herself back, she took a handkerchief from her purse and brushed her face.

"I'm going to tell you that every day, from here on out," he promised.

"What—about marriage?"

"About being wonderful," he corrected. They laughed and moved to the door, where she turned and faced him.

"You'll have to go now," she said gravely.

"I know, but I don't want to." She stared at him and he saw her mental tussle.

"I don't want you to either," she confesssed. "You'll probably think me a vixen when I tell you I wish tonight could be just like last time—every single second of it. I'm fighting with myself not to invite you in, and you've got to help me. You've got to go, Joe."

"I love you, and because of that I will," he promised. "Kiss me . . . once."

"Yes." They kissed again, tenderly at first, then more passionately. He moved his hands down her body, encircled her waist and held her tight, feeling the thump of her heart. She strained against him and began to murmur softly, so faintly he scarcely heard the words.

"I love you, love you," she murmured. He stopped the flow of words with his lips and they clung passionately to each other. Stark felt his new-found resolve slipping. The girl in his arms was wonderful, wonderful. He kissed her again, filled with ardor and felt her respond.

After a while she pushed herself back, saying in a monotone, "All right, I don't care what you think. I want you to stay. You've made me do this. Now you can come in, Joe."

He felt instantly contrite. "Please, I'm no stronger than you are. It wasn't deliberate. You've got to believe that. Now go to bed, I'm going to my room."

She stared disbelievingly at him, then moved into his arms and sobbed against his shoulder.

After a while he returned to the Hawker house.

❀ nine

STARK AWAKENED to the sound of someone knocking at the door. He blinked a few times to shake the sleep from his eyes, then scrambled to his feet and pulled on his clothes.

"Tuan!" Gurko Singh's voice bore a note of urgency and he pulled open the door.

"What's wrong?"

"Trouble, Tuan." The Bengali pointed toward the infirmary.

"What kind of trouble?" he demanded.

"Big trouble."

"Let's go, he snapped, thinking he was getting nowhere with the questions.

The sun rested just above the horizon, big and red, and from the jungles the howl of monkeys heralded the dawn. He hurried to keep up as the Bengali headed toward the infirmary with giant strides. To Stark's dismay, he rounded the building going toward the cottages in the rear. Lord! Stark broke into a run. Coming around the corner he saw first Suzanne and Yoshi, then a figure sprawled at their feet. The tan slacks and gay sport shirt told him it was Hawker. Suzanne turned to face him, her eyes stricken.

"What happened?" he demanded.

"It's Mike—he's dead," she answered. He bent down and examined the superintendent's body and seeing no wound, carefully rolled it over. A slender steel dart protruded just below the left shoulder. He reached down and pulled it out, thinking the act senseless. Hawker was dead —quite dead.

Looking up, he asked quietly, "Who found him?"

"Madju," Yoshi answered.

He switched his gaze to the nurse's face. It appeared calm, imperturbable; he saw no sign that only hours before she had been lover to the man who now lay dead at her feet—none of emotion, neither joy nor grief. Just blankness. *The East, the hidden East,* he thought.

"Who's Madju?" he asked brusquely.

"One of the attendants in the infirmary. He was coming to open it, and found him."

"Then he called you?"

"Yes." Stark switched his gaze to Suzanne.

"I heard him shout and came out," she explained.

"Heard who shout—Madju?"

"Yes."

Stark glanced at the body again. "We'd better carry him inside."

"Poor Selinda," Suzanne murmured.

"I sent one of the boys for her," Yoshi said. He started to reply, checked the words and stooping, lifted the dead man's body and carried it to the infirmary, where he laid it on one of the surgical tables. A quick patter of feet came from the porch and Selinda burst through the doorway. She had thrown on a white wrap and her face looked stricken.

"Mike!" The word came in a plaintive scream as she stared at her husband's body. There was a momentary tableau during which Stark found himself faintly puzzled by her evident grief; it was broken as she threw her hands to her face and began sobbing violently.

"I'll get her a sedative," Yoshi said professionally, moving away. Stark found himself doubly puzzled: he had not expected such a display of grief from Selinda; neither had he expected the calm acceptance of Hawker's death from the nurse. More important, why had Hawker been murdered? He shuffled the reasons in his mind.

Item. Hodges hated him, envied him, and the dead man allegedly had had an affair with Hodges' wife. *Item.* Saito, for Hawker was the key man in plans to demolish the plant. *Item.* Yoshi—for reasons which only she knew. *Item, item, item* . . . there were any number of reasons why Hawker could have been killed. The problem would be to find the actual reason—that and the identity of the killer. It looked like the Driscoll case all over again. Selinda pulled her hands from her face and stared glassily at the body. Her eyes were wet, glazed with pain.

"Why? Why?" she moaned dully. She covered her face again and gave way to racking sobs. For a moment there was no other sound in the room—only that of her grief. Stark caught Suzanne's eye and she smiled bravely back.

"You'd better get some rest," he advised her.

Instead, she moved to Selinda's side and placed a hand on her arm, saying, "I'll take you to the house."

"Take this first," Yoshi ordered, returning with a glass of liquid. Selinda mutely accepted the proffered glass, stared at it, then drank. Afterward Suzanne led her back to the house.

When they were gone, Stark swung toward the nurse, saying tersely, "Make whatever arrangements you usually make in a case like this. I'll tell Hodges."

"I'll take care of everything," Yoshi replied stonily. Her eyes swung down to the body again before she turned away. Like flint, Stark thought. She had a hardness he hadn't suspected. He filed the information away and went outside, hesitating before turning toward the Hodges' house. Martha answered his knock.

"Jasper in?" he asked perfunctorily.

"He's asleep. Won't you come in?" She stepped aside, eying him curiously as he entered. She had thrown on a faded blue bathrobe and he suspected she wore nothing under it. Her eyes appeared heavy with sleep. She asked quietly, "Trouble?"

"Yes, Hawker's dead."

"Mike—dead?" She uttered the words incredulously, staring at him.

"Blowgun," he explained.

"Oh, how terrible. I'll get Jasper right away." She hurried into the other room, and after a moment he heard Hodges' startled voice, then the creak of the bed and movement. Hodges emerged from the room still tucking in his shirt. His eyes were red-rimmed and inflamed.

"What's this about Hawker?" he demanded.

"Murdered—with a blowgun," Stark stated, thinking he could eliminate the man as a suspect. Hodges had slept drunkenly all night.

"Christ!" He glanced back at his wife. "I'd better call Vandervoort, let him know, then get in touch with the boys." His voice became complaining. "This is a hell of a time for this to happen."

"Any time's a bad time," Stark snapped, trying to conceal his irritation.

"I'll get you some coffee first," Martha cut in.

"Get Stark some; I've got work to do," her husband snapped. He stamped out the door without looking back.

"Care for a cup?" she asked.

"No thanks, I'll take a rain check."

He followed Hodges from the house and walked slowly toward the office. A few minutes later Hodges came out.

"I told Vandervoort," he said abruptly. "They're having trouble with the coolies."

"Deserting?"

"Uh-huh." Hodges stared over the compound. "Well, I'm running this place now. I'm going to get things rolling."

"Rolling how?" Stark challenged, not liking the other's tone.

Hodges jutted his jaw forward and snapped, "Getting things done—running this place the way I damn well want to run it."

Stark controlled his temper. "Well, that's your prerogative, but it seems to me your course of action is pretty well mapped."

"Is it, Stark?" Hodges laughed nastily. "Maybe Hawker didn't give a damn for human life, but I do."

"What do you propose to do?" Stark asked evenly.

"Get our people ready to evacuate. Get the power launches standing by. Get the things we need. Christ, we can't swim naked up that river. Hawker yapped about an escape route but do you see any preparations?"

"I happen to know they're made," Stark said quietly. "The Vandervoort group's coming up the river. We join them, go upstream to Telukbetang, down to Sunda Strait. When the Plaju refineries blow, they alert the Navy. The rest is arranged."

"Wait for Vandervoort . . ." Hodges sneered and turned away.

Stark watched him retreat with narrowing eyes, then saw Suzanne and walked to meet her.

"Selinda's sleeping," she explained. "The sedative Yoshi gave her took effect immediately."

"That's good." He took her arm as they walked to her house. Inside, he tenderly kissed her. She returned it warmly, then broke away, saying in mock severity, "Just one. I'm putting you on a ration. I can't stand the strain."

"So now it's rations? Golly, I hope you don't do that after we're married."

"Of course not, silly. Why should I ration anything then?" She caught his look and blushed, saying accusingly, "You're always looking for hidden meanings in what I say."

"I am. How about another kiss?"

"You're on a ration."

"Of course, this is tomorrow's allotment."

"Tomorrow . . ." Her face grew sober.

"Maybe I'd better collect next year's."

"Joe, you fool." She moved into his arms and kissed him long and hard. When she moved her face away, he saw the wetness in her eyes. She tried a game smile. "I keep thinking of these tomorrows—how many of them have we left, Joe?"

He laughed reassuringly. "Well, there are three hundred and sixty-five in a year, and if you multiply that by about forty . . ."

"You're my fool," she said. "Now you'll have to go. I have things to do."

"All right, but I want to see you in a while."

"What for?" she asked curiously.

"To collect my ration for the day after tomorrow."

"Joe Stark, you go home." She pushed him out the door.

The break came sooner than Stark expected.

Walking toward the Hawker garden, he saw the pickup truck speeding back from the powerhouse and paused to wait. It slid to a halt alongside him and Texas Smith leaped out, his face angry. He wore a holstered .45 revolver that appeared ludicrously large against his small frame. Stark had the sudden knowledge he knew how to use it. He wore the gun too carelessly. Hodges and Pete Holden piled out of the truck more slowly.

"What's up?" Stark asked tersely.

"Hodges—" Texas Smith jerked a thumb toward the new superintendent—"wants to get the evacuation started —blow the works today."

"Those are my orders," Hodges snarled, glaring at Stark. He swung his eyes back to Texas Smith, a malevolent glint in them as he weighed his subordinate. "Smith doesn't seem to think he's working for me."

"I'm not buying it," Smith snapped. "Hawker made it clear we were to wait for the Plaju people to blow the works."

"You can't seem to get it in your mind that Hawker ain't running this place any more," Hodges retorted angrily.

"Damn right I can't."

"You're right, Smith," Stark cut in coldly.

Hodges spun toward him, eyes glittering. "I can't see that you're concerned," he rasped.

"No?"

Hodges said evenly. "You have no authority here—not a damn bit."

"Whaddya mean, he's from the head office," Smith snapped.

"Head office . . ." Hodges laughed nastily. "Christ, Stark, you're ONI and everyone with any brains knows it. You haven't the least bit of authority as far as this plant is concerned. This isn't government, or didn't you know?"

87

Stark caught Smith's startled expression. "Where did you hear that?" he challenged.

"About your being ONI?"

"Yes."

"Well, I can't rightly say," Hodges replied calmly, "but the word gets around. You want me to give you a bit of advice?"

"Go ahead," Stark said bluntly.

"You're a dead duck," Hodges snapped. "If you're smart, you'll keep your nose out of my business and scram."

"Is that a threat?" Stark's voice dropped to a low, sharp edges and Hodges involuntarily took a backward step.

"No, it's not a threat, but look what happened to Driscoll. The point is, I won't be responsible for your safety."

"Who in hell's asking you to?" Stark caustically asked.

Hodges flushed. "Furthermore, I don't want any more of your damned interference."

Texas Smith came to life. "Why were you sent here?" he asked Stark directly.

The ONI man saw no hostility in the dark eyes and said calmly, "To work with Hawker—make certain the orders on demolishing the plant were carried out."

"Then you do have authority?" Smith pursued.

"I have authority," he answered calmly.

"Authority, hell," Hodges rasped.

Smith spun toward him. "This is war," he stated, his eyes hooded and alert.

Hodges sneered. "So what?"

"So I'm seeing that the order's carried out." Smith patted his holster.

"You're threatening me?" Hodges blustered.

"If you put it that way, yes." Smith's eyes were angry.

"You're through with this company," Hodges retorted, turning to the men. "I'll blackball you from here to hell-and-gone."

"We'll talk about that later," Smith answered, and swung toward Holden. "Are you with me, Pete?"

Stark moved his eyes to the driller's face. Tall and gangling, he had the look of a man who had lived too many years under the tropic sun. He wore his .45 holstered snug against his hip.

"Reckon I am," he replied nonchalantly.

"You're through, too," Hodges blurted.

"Am I?" Holden laughed mirthlessly.

"You'd better get back to the powerhouse," Stark advised, eying Smith. He knew the invasion was a dead certainty and wanted to say so, but orders were orders. Besides, Smith and Holden knew it, too. Maybe neither had ever been soldiers but somewhere the adherence to orders had been ingrained deeply within them. He was thankful for that. He switched his glance to Hodges. "You too— you'd better play it straight, or else . . ."

"Or else what?" Hodges cut in.

"Or else I get suddenly patriotic," Smith interjected, slapping the holster again. "You don't think I'm reluctant, do you?"

Holden laughed again and climbed back into the truck. Hodges stared at Smith before he abruptly turned and followed. Smith's eyelid drooped in a slow wink, then he crawled into the driver's seat and started the engine. Stark watched the truck bounce across the field, thinking Smith was a good man. Right now he wished he had a score like him.

❀ ten

JOE STARK flicked the ashes from his cigarette, watching Yoshi Kusaka's small cottage from the shadow of a tree. A lamp beamed through a window, throwing a splash of yellow light across the ground; occasionally he saw movement behind the curtain. Shifting positions, he glanced at the sky.

The moon rode low in the east, occasionally obscured by a passing cloud, but the earlier threat of rain had passed. Mosquito wings sang, competing with the bright chirrup of cicadas, and a pungent odor pervaded the air. A faint red glow far across the field told where the furnaces of the cracking plant spewed their flame into the sky. To the other side, just off the river road, stretched the wide fields of lalang grass, separated from one another by clumps of jungle—the tiger fields. He shivered slightly and glanced at his watch, surprised to find that it was but a few minutes after eight.

This was the night—if Selinda Hawker was right—that Yoshi made her furtive trips to Telukta; he intended to discover why. His thoughts flicked back to Selinda. She had kept to her room since her husband's death, served only by Obak, although Suzanne had visited her several times, reporting she seemed over the worst of the shock.

During the day a Dutch police official had arrived, asked a few questions, and had departed. Now Hawker's body reposed on a slab in a dingy Palembang funeral parlor; he would be buried the following day.

Stark thought the end oddly fitting for the brutal boss of the oil empire—strong men had a way of being buried at alien ends of the earth; he would find such a spot for himself someday. Not that he was in a hurry. He smiled grimly at the thought. He had too much yet to see and do. The world was a treasure house.

He stared at the shimmering stars and the field beyond, black and empty, irritably thinking there was much he didn't know. Selinda, an enigma . . . She could be ice or flame. Demure, bold, guileless, wanton—yes, completely wanton—and also a consummate actress. He recalled the scene at the dinner table: she had played the role of a perfect wife, acting as if Stark were exactly what he was supposed to be—a guest, a VIP from the main office, and nothing more. Yet she had literally gone there from his arms. Despite that, her grief appeared genuine. Perhaps in her own way she had really loved her brutal, hulking and

90

equally faithless husband, he thought. He'd seen stranger things.

Item. She had rightfully called the shot on Yoshi and Hawker. To that extent he couldn't afford to write off her words as meaningless. But Yoshi herself posed another problem—an equally baffling one. She had welcomed Hawker to her bed, yet had displayed no emotion at his walking from that same bed to his death. He tussled with the problems. Well, perhaps tonight he'd find some answers.

Yoshi's lamp blinked out; he stood very still. Seconds later her door opened and she slipped outside, glancing furtively around before striking out toward the road that led to Telukta. He allowed her to get a sufficient lead before following, walking silently and avoiding the splotches of moonlight which here and there filtered through the trees. She reached the river road and took it without looking back.

Stark quickly discovered that it was a road only in the sense that it was a cleared area stretching between swamp and jungles. Rutted and for the most part muddy, it appeared little more than a wide trail. Remembering the tiger field, he patted his automatic, admiring the courage of the girl he followed. Yet she moved with an assurance that told him she had made the journey many times.

Once she stopped, glancing back, and he froze, waiting until she resumed her way before following. When the road began to wind, he closed the distance between them. After a while the trees began to thin out; he saw a sprinkling of lights in the distance and his nostrils caught the agreeable scent of burning resinous gum.

Telukta had grown haphazardly to meet its own peculiar requirements. Starting with swamp and stilt-rooted houses, gradually it ascended to form a small highland plateau. The rise in the ground was the main reason for the hamlet's existence, for it was here the wealthy Chinese *taukehs* and Indian merchant princes came to build their homes, secure from the swamp waters which during the rainy season swirled through the jungle swamps below.

91

He passed an inlet crowded with houseboats and sampans, climbed a winding lane and came to the main street, a muddy avenue ushered in by a bright-tiled Buddhist temple that reminded him of Siam. Beyond loomed two Moslem minarets. Most of the houses had steep-pitched roofs of straw thatch, although a few were of corrugated iron and others of tile. Several of the homes were quite European in style.

Yoshi turned into a side street and he hurried to catch up, rounding the corner just in time to see her turn up a walk leading to a house set among some tall trees. His mind ticked off the fact the house was built of brick and timber, possessed a balcony, and definitely was better than its neighboring structures. The upper windows were dark but lamplight came from what he judged would be the front room. Not a native home, he thought. He heard her knock.

When the door opened, emitting a shaft of yellow light, he caught sight of the bent form of an old man. He had a glimpse of white hair, and odd dressing gown, before Yoshi passed into the house, closing the door behind her. Something stirred in Stark's mind—a fast sorting of faces, dress, nationality, a kaleidoscope of places and people; with it came a realization the aged figure had been Japanese. How he knew, he wasn't sure. Perhaps the clothes . . .

He lit a cigarette and settled back to wait, swinging his eyes to search the narrow street. Gleaming lamps shining through gaily curtained windows, houses fronted with grasses and tropical shrubs, picket fences, cobblestone walks and occasional verandas aglow with Japanese lanterns—it could be a street from almost anywhere, he thought. Strange scents filled the air—resinous gum, cooking fish, spices, incense. He relaxed, waiting.

Five minutes passed, then ten. He started to glance at his watch again when a warning bell rang in his brain; he jerked alert, sensing danger without knowing its source. His scalp prickled and he withdrew the automatic, his eyes searching the street and its shadows.

Remaining absolutely motionless, he watched and listened. From somewhere came a wailing Hindu song, the bark of a dog. His imagination? He didn't think so. The alert had been too sudden, too strong. The empty street was an illusion. Forgetful of Yoshi, he kept his attention attuned to the night, only his perfect training and long exposure to such situations keeping him from moving.

The alarm came again; he recognized it as a warning set off by some sound or sight subconsciously perceived, to which some inner sense had placed a tag reading *danger*.

Slowly he moved his head, cutting the shadows into blocks and searching them one by one. Movement in the periphery of his eye caused him to whirl; he saw the glint of light on the blade of a parang.

Hurling himself to one side, he stumbled, brought up the automatic and released the safety. A dark figure darted forward, lifted the blade and he fired. Red flame spat from the barrel, lanced the night, and a crashing roar echoed through the streets.

Leaping to his feet, he caught sight of several moving figures and crouched, holding the automatic at waist level while trying to see on all sides of him at once.

A shadow rushed out of the darkness and he fired; the figure reeled and fell. Cursing softly, he fired at another shadow. The night erupted with movement as half a dozen slim figures converged on him. A savage blow to the side of his head sent him reeling backward and he fell, struggling to lift the automatic.

Joe Stark, watch out! The cry came from his brain as a Malay brandishing a wicked-looking blade leaped astride his legs. He lashed up with his foot and caught the man in the groin. A howl split the night and Stark struggled erect, catching an arm, breaking it with a vicious twist, jamming the weapon into another face and firing point-blank. Pandemonium broke loose.

A familiar bellow sounded near-by and a giant figure leaped to his side swinging a wavy-bladed kris. One of the attackers went down with a gurgling scream. *Gurko! Gurko Singh!*

93

The Bengali's blade sliced off a hand swinging a parang while Stark grabbed another assailant by the throat and smashed his head against the cobblestones. Silence came abruptly and he whirled toward Singh. His attackers melted into the night as quietly as they had come, the patter of their feet dying in the distance. Doors were opening, throwing narrow shafts of lamplight across the street, and he heard the chatter of excited voices.

"Tuan, are you hurt?" The Bengali anxiously studied him.

"A knot on the noggin . . ." His eyes swept the bodies ringing them, then shifted toward the door of the house where Yoshi had gone. It stood open; he saw the aged figure outlined against the lamplight, staring into the darkness, but of Yoshi he saw no sign. A few of the more daring had come out of their houses and he heard the clamor of voices from farther down the street.

"Let's get out of here," he rasped.

They raced toward the opposite corner, the Bengali leading the way. He twisted between some houses, crossed another street and finally halted near the main thoroughfare. Panting, Stark stared at his companion.

"You got here in the nick of time," he said, searching the Bengali's face. "You followed me?"

"Yes, Tuan."

"Why?"

"Missee Ebell say so," he answered simply.

"Miss Ebell ordered you to follow me?"

"She say Tuan get in trouble," Gurko explained.

"Do you always follow me?" Stark asked carefully.

"Yes, Tuan."

Stark laughed, thinking he was one hell of an ONI operator. Six and a half feet of shadow on his trail and he'd never suspected it. Durling would frown. The humor of it struck him and he laughed aloud.

"Well, it turned out to be a great idea," he said.

Next morning Stark headed toward the infirmary in an ugly mood. The blow above his ear had resulted in a

94

tender, painful lump; more than that was the knowledge he had come near death from the hands of his as yet unknown adversary. Only Gurko's timely intervention had saved him.

He laid the assault at Yoshi's door, even though he realized she couldn't have known he was shadowing her. *(But Selinda knew. She tacitly had suggested it.)* More probable, the owner of the house Yoshi had visited maintained a guard for just such purposes. With the house that securely guarded, the visit was more than a social call, as she might claim.

The old man was Saito. The facts pointed in that direction. If so, Yoshi was a Japanese agent. Hodges knew he was ONI. How? Stark resurrected the probable events. Yoshi must have dug the information from Hawker, spread it in an attempt to make Stark's position as a company VIP untenable. She could have masterminded the deaths of Driscoll, Hawker. . . .

Both Yoshi and Dr. Ebell were working in the infirmary when he entered. The latter's slender face, haggard and gray with fatigue, bore testimony to the long hours he had spent in the field hospital. Yoshi appeared crisply cool in a fresh white uniform. Ebell searched his face appraisingly before concentrating on the lump above his ear.

"Trouble?" he asked quietly.

"A bit." Stark stared at Yoshi and asked bluntly: "Why did you go to Telukta last night?"

A startled look crossed her face before being replaced by a composed mask. "I don't believe it's any of your business," she stated coolly.

"What's all this?" Ebell snapped testily. His lips drew into a tight line.

"Yoshi went to Telukta last night," Stark said briefly. "I followed her." He didn't mention the fight.

"You had no right to follow me," she exclaimed. Their eyes clashed.

"I agree with her, Stark." The doctor weighed the ONI man thoughtfully. "Don't you think she's entitled to a private life of her own—something outside this infirmary?"

95

"In this case, no."

"Why not?" Ebell challenged.

"This is war, a time of crisis. We've had three murders."

"Three?"

"Tombuk," Stark supplied. He smiled faintly. "He was human, too."

"What has that to do with me?" Yoshi exclaimed.

"That's what I intend to find out."

"I think you're going too far," Ebell stated. "Murder is a matter for the police."

"There's more than murder involved." Stark contemplated the doctor. "We have this plant on our hands—"

"Well," Ebell cut in.

"We damn well don't want it delivered to the Japanese," Stark ended. Ebell's face grew stern.

"So you've chosen to persecute Yoshi," he accused.

"I'm persecuting no one. I'm just asking questions."

"And if she doesn't choose to answer them?"

"I don't choose to answer them," Yoshi stated loftily.

"No?" Stark narrowed his eyes. "I saw the house you went to, saw who was there. . . ." He didn't finish, watching intently for a change of expression. A shadow of flickering doubt crossed her face and almost as quickly passed.

Looking annoyed, Ebell said, "Personally, I don't like this cloak-and-dagger stuff. I don't know why Yoshi went to Telukta but I'm sure it's her own business, and I'd prefer you didn't bother her while she's here at the clinic."

Stark suppressed his irritation.

"Thank you, Doctor," Yoshi said. Her eyes flashing angrily at Stark, she turned and left the room.

Stark took a parting shot at the doctor. "Your certainty's going to trip you up," he declared.

When Ebell didn't reply, he left.

They buried Mike Hawker that afternoon.

Selinda came from the house clothed in a simple dark cotton dress, a black veil covering her hair. Stark helped her into the rear seat of a battered company sedan and got in beside her while Gurko slipped behind the wheel. The Hodges and Texas Smith followed in a second car; a third held Dr. Ebell, his daughter and the nurse, Yoshi. The latter looked cool and aloof. Pete Holden remained behind to watch over the powerhouse.

The clouds had gathered again, heavy and dark, with occasional drifts of rain spattering against the windshield. The wind picked up, blowing in from the strait, bringing the promise of a *sumatra*. Selinda stared straight ahead, her slender face taut with strain.

The small procession splashed along the jungle road, wound through Telukta, crossed a swampy plain and entered Palembang. Gurko Singh stopped in front of a drab-appearing funeral parlor, and the other cars pulled up behind.

Stark got out and held open the door for Selinda while his eyes sought Suzanne. Ebell had told her of the episode in the infirmary and when he had seen her later, she appeared quite stiff and cool, saying, "Really, Joe, it sounds ridiculous. Yoshi is my friend."

Now she marched past him staring straight ahead. As the rain began to slant down, he hurried inside. The small chapel contained half a dozen wooden benches and a dais, on which sat a pulpit and Hawker's casket, the latter a lacquered wooden box with gold trim. A large vase filled with an odd mixture of orchids, rhododendron and other jungle blooms filled one corner, and from an adjoining room came the scratchy recording of a funeral dirge.

Stark sat in the front of the room next to Selinda, conscious that the portly Vandervoort, his wife and a sprinkling of other people had entered. When the music ended, the minister, who also was the mortician, entered and took his place behind the pulpit. Dutch, short and stout, he had a round face, bald pate, and spoke broken English. He led in a short prayer, then delivered the eulogy.

Michael Hawker, he declaimed, had been a great man, loved and revered by both his countrymen and natives alike. He had raised oil temples in the jungles, brought wealth to his adopted land, left a legacy of wisdom and hope. He had departed leaving a loving and faithful wife, a memory that would endure as a monument in the hearts of his friends. He said more of the same while the rain drummed against the corrugated roof, repeating himself as if waiting for it to slacken. Finally it did. Following a brief prayer, the scratchy recording came on again.

The minister nodded and Selinda rose, walking to the coffin and staring in. She left, dabbing at her eyes. One by one the others paid their last respects, then the minister shut the lid of the casket.

Acting as pallbearers, Vandervoort and a man Stark hadn't met before joined the men from Sumatra Independent. They carried the casket outside, laying it in the back of an ancient hearse, then the funeral procession moved through the muddy streets of Palembang to a small graveyard on a hill at the town's edge.

The minister delivered another graveside sermon, brief this time as the rain was slanting down, after which the casket was lowered and the funeral party returned to Sumatra Independent.

There Selinda uttered her first words: "Thank you, Joe Stark," she said, as he saw her to the house.

Yoshi came to Stark's room that night.

Preparing for bed, he heard voices outside, followed by a light tapping at his door. He opened it and Gurko Singh, his face expressionless, stepped aside and he saw her.

"May I come in?" she inquired in a low voice.

"Certainly." He glanced around. "I'm afraid the room's a bit of a mess."

"That's quite all right."

Closing the door behind her, he watched her curiously. She wore a flowered Japanese kimono, but had removed the customary comb from her hair. Reed slippers encased her small feet.

"Have a chair," he invited. "How can I help you?" He walked over and sat on the edge of the bed, facing her, sensing she was troubled.

"It's about last night," she said.

98

"What about last night?"

"I want you to know that you're wrong about me." She stared calmly at him but he had a feeling that terror lay in her mind, perhaps in a state of suspension, but none the less terror.

"Wrong about what?" he asked quietly.

"You think I'm . . . a spy." She uttered the last word with a slight gasp of agitation.

"I didn't say that."

"No, but that's why you're checking . . . following me."

"Well, supposing you tell me about it," he offered. "Perhaps we can iron out everything."

Hesitating, she spoke calmly: "I go to visit my father."

"Why didn't you say so before?" he demanded.

"He's Japanese . . . an enemy alien in the eyes of the Dutch. You know that. They don't know where he is," she added.

"You think they'd bother him?"

"Of course, and he's old and sick—too old to live in one of their concentration camps."

"They don't bother you," he pointed out. She bit her lip.

"I'm different. I was born here."

"And he wasn't?"

"No, he was born in Tokyo."

He mulled the information, conscious of her eyes. She sat with her hands folded, looking very composed, only the flickering of her eyelids portraying her nervousness. He thought she looked quite lovely. Finally he said, "There are other things."

"Like what?" She stiffened slightly.

He said carefully, "Some information has gotten around that could only come from Hawker." A startled expression crossed her face and she compressed her lips, not answering. He added bluntly: "You were his lover."

"No, not that," she denied vehemently.

"Don't lie. I know better," he replied quietly.

A bitter look came to her face and she spoke in a low

99

tone. "I gave myself to him, yes. He would come to my room at night. But I hated him, hated him. . . ." Her eyes, dark and brooding, met his.

"Why?" he asked.

"To keep him quiet." Her tongue edged her lips, and she added: "He knew."

"About your father?"

"Yes."

Stark asked wonderingly, "He used that information to blackmail you?"

"Yes." She repeated the word in a flat monotone, then stared defiantly at him and stated: "Perhaps you think that strange, but among my people a father is very revered. It was not too great a price to pay for his silence."

"Did Hawker ever mention me?" he asked.

"No." Her hands weren't quite steady.

"But you've heard things?"

"Yes."

"From where?" he demanded.

"One of the Malays." She looked away.

"Which one?"

"Tombuk."

"What exactly did he say?"

"He said you were some sort of policeman."

"Have you repeated that?"

"Never," she said forcefully.

He changed the subject, asking gently, "You came here tonight because you're afraid of me?"

"Yes, and to assure your silence."

"I would have to know more about your father."

She watched him steadily. "What can I say? He is old, infirm, never leaves the house. He spends his days in meditation, and with his books. How could such a man be dangerous? It's just that he's living in an age of suspicion and hostility, a hatred of everything Japanese," she ended bitterly.

"So on your word alone, you wish me to accept that?"

"I wish to assure your silence." Her eyes didn't waver as he stared at her, puzzled.

"How?" he asked finally.

She smiled bitterly. "Like I assured Hawker's silence—with my body."

He closed his eyes, feeling a flash of pain and pity for the slim girl opposite him.

"That won't be necessary," he said. "I believe you."

⚙ eleven

STARK RECEIVED his first indication of real trouble early the following morning when Jasper Hodges came speeding back along the road from the powerhouse and braked the truck to a fast stop in front of the office. Stark hurried down from the veranda as he leaped from the cab.

"Trouble?" he asked.

"Plenty," Hodges snapped. "The dynamite lines to the cracking plant and foundry were sabotaged last night, and Christ knows what else. On top of that, another batch of coolies deserted. I'd better call Vandervoort and see where we stand." He pulled a red bandanna from his pocket to wipe the sweat from his face. Stark felt a momentary misgiving.

"I'd better go back with you, give a hand," he offered.

Hodges stared indecisively at him, finally protesting, "We need someone to cover the office."

"Suzanne can do that. I'll call her."

Hodges wavered, staring dully across the compound. "Okay, I guess that'll work," he agreed.

Stark watched him trudge heavily up the office steps before turning toward the infirmary. Yoshi met him at the entrance, smiling faintly, but the smile was friendly and he felt better.

101

"Suzanne around?" he asked.

"I believe she's at the house."

He thanked her, went out the rear way and knocked at the doctor's door. Suzanne answered. She appeared somewhat reserved and failed to invite him in. After he quickly explained the situation, she said briefly, "I'll be right over."

When she turned away without waiting for his answer, he shrugged stoically and trudged back to the infirmary, where he found Yoshi preparing bandages.

Studying her slim figure, he said, "Suzanne's a little unhappy with me."

"Oh?" She eyed him demurely.

"Square me with her, will you?"

"Square you?" She laughed, a tinkling, bell-like sound, and he grinned. Studying him amusedly, she promised: "I'll try."

"Great . . . Yoshi." He watched her levelly, catching a flash of dancing devils in her eyes before she said, "I'll do my best, Joe."

"Wonderful." He left the infirmary, glad to be on first-name relations with the Japanese girl; a step in the right direction, he thought. He should have taken the cue from Suzanne and her father, gotten to know her sooner. Still, he had to suspect—that was his job. Seeing Hodges emerge from the office, he quickened his step.

"Vandervoort has things under pretty good control, but he says they're having plenty of trouble at the other plants —sabotage and wholesale desertions," the superintendent informed him. "There's hell to pay."

"We'll stop that here," Stark promised.

"Yeah, but that's not the worst. They got a radio report that the Japs are moving in for the kill." His face flushed. "Damn you, Stark, I told you."

"They haven't hit yet," he snapped grimly. "We hold out till they do. Those are the orders."

"Damned poor orders," Hodges sneered. He sucked at his lip. "Vandervoort's calling a meeting of the key people of all the plants—something about synchronizing the demolition programs and tying down our escape procedures. He wants to work out everything tonight. I'll run over."

Agreeing it was a good idea, Stark followed him into the truck. Suzanne came around from the rear of the infirmary just as they started toward the powerhouse road. Stark waved. She let a few seconds elapse before responding, but he felt better; she couldn't be too annoyed.

They found Texas Smith guarding the main ignition switches. He explained that Holden had taken a couple of natives out to repair the damage.

"We're going to have our hands full," he added. "We're going to have to check every line running to the reservoirs, foundry and cracking plant. I'd do it now except . . ." He stopped talking and glanced meaningfully across the room toward Talo, the *mandur,* who was directing a group of coolies in the task of moving some equipment. The Malay wore a parang that appeared huge in comparison with his slim body.

"I'm here to help," Stark answered, glad to see that Smith packed his .45. He glanced around the powerhouse; a brick structure, it had been selected as the key point in the demolition program because of its central position and relative invulnerability. "I'm pretty fair with ignition systems," he finished.

"Good, if Jasper wants to hold down the fort . . ." Smith glanced questioningly at the superintendent.

"I'll take over." Hodges began paging through a stack of magazines cluttering a desk.

Smith got a couple of splicing tools before they went outside to join Holden's crew. The latter had already repaired the lines running to the foundry and cracking plant and now was checking the score of lines which ran to the oil reservoirs.

"They're cut, too," he announced grimly, when they reached his side.

Stark felt his apprehensions rise; everything was going wrong. Millions of gallons of fuel were at stake—fuel badly needed by the Japanese Navy. He could consider

103

anything less than total demolition of the huge plant a failure—one that couldn't be explained to the agate-eyed Durling. The urgency of time rushed over him.

They worked steadily throughout the day, checking each line and repairing those that were damaged. Finished, they returned to the powerhouse, where Smith, Holden and Hodges went into a confab to set the watch for the night.

Stark saw Talo checking some gear at the far side of the room and walked over to join him. The *mandur* glanced up at his approach, then straightened respectfully, his eyes watchful. Stark had the impression that a tiger lay concealed in the man's dark, slender body; it had the look of a coiled steel spring.

Scanning the Malay's face, he said, "I'm curious over why so many of your people are deserting." When Talo didn't answer, he prompted: "Do you know why?"

"Yes, Tuan." The answer caught him by surprise, and he thought, *At least the man's honest.*

"Why are they leaving?" he pressed.

"Trouble, Tuan." Talo shifted his eyes.

"What kind of trouble?" he demanded. The *mandur* looked faintly uncomfortable and Stark repeated the question.

This time Talo stared directly at him, saying in a low voice, "The Jap man, Tuan."

"Jap man?" Stark failed to conceal his surprise. "What Jap man?"

Talo shrugged.

"Then how do you know it's a Jap man?" he demanded.

"Talo hear," the *mandur* replied.

"Hear what?" Stark pressed the point, feeling he had the Malay off balance. If he could crack him . . . The *mandur* glanced beseechingly toward Hodges before reluctantly bringing back his eyes.

"Talo hear Jap man want coolies to go home," he confessed. Stark felt a surge of elation.

"You know this man?"

The *mandur* hesitated, studying his hands, and suddenly

104

Stark knew the answer. *Talo did know.* He could see it in the man's hesitancy, his slow deliberation.

Finally the Malay lifted his head, and replied, "Maybe not Jap man."

"What do you mean by that?" Stark rasped, thinking Talo was giving him double-talk. The Malay shifted his feet uneasily.

"Maybe not Jap man. Maybe Jap lady," he said.

"What?" Stark stared at him, his thoughts a sudden jumble. "What lady?"

Talo said carefully: "Maybe Yoshi."

"Yoshi!" he exclaimed.

"Yes, Tuan," the *mandur* said firmly.

Stark's voice became ice. "How does she do it?"

"Do what, Tuan?"

"Spread the word."

"When boys get sick, boys go to sick house. Then Yoshi talk to them. Yoshi say tuans bad, Jap man good—Malay boys should go home, back to villages."

Stark glanced around. The others were still in a huddle. Yoshi—he remembered the way she had looked when she had come to his room. She had sounded completely honest, without guile. Mentally he had crossed her off as a suspect. The image of the aged Japanese he'd seen in Telukta flashed through his mind. Yoshi's father . . . He smiled grimly, bringing his eyes back to the *mandur* and remembering that Selinda had vouched for his loyalty.

"Have you told that to anyone else?" he demanded.

"No, Tuan."

"Why not?"

A faint smile touched Talo's lips, so faint Stark barely detected it.

"No one asked, Tuan."

So, no one had asked! The *mandur* had held the key all along, a key that hadn't unlocked any doors simply because no one had asked. He cursed himself for a fool, thinking he should have known that such people never volunteered information. They listened, observed and

105

seldom talked. Hawker and the others should have known, too.

He became aware of a faint suspicion nagging at the back of his mind: Talo's admission had come too readily. Casually he searched the Malay's face, finding absolutely nothing; the *mandur* wore it like a mask, and like a mask it came devoid of all emotion. Selinda, as an actress, might well take second billing to Yoshi, he thought. The Japanese girl might well be playing a superb role.

"Keep quiet about this," he commanded.

"Yes, Tuan."

Stark shot him a last glance before rejoining the others. He returned to the office with Hodges in the fall of the evening, his thoughts jumbled. A few days ago all trails pointed toward Yoshi, then had turned away. He had turned them away, he corrected. Now the spotlight had picked her out again. He pondered it before turning his thoughts to the powerhouse—in his mind, the key spot.

Due to the scheduled meeting Hodges was to attend at the Plaju refinery, Holden had the watch for the night while Texas Smith had volunteered to patrol the lonely reservoir area. Stark felt thankful for the latter's presence on the job. Despite his runt-sized figure, he pegged the Texan for a powerhouse. He didn't feel so certain about the taciturn Holden.

Hodges parked in front of the office and Suzanne hurried down from the veranda.

"Vandervoort called again. The meeting has been set back till ten o'clock," she said. Hodges grumbled and she turned to Stark, saying, "I'm glad you're back. Dad's going to the field hospital and I want to make sure he gets supper."

"I'll walk you home," he quickly offered. Neither of them spoke until they reached the rear of the infirmary. Then he stopped her and asked bluntly, "You're angry with me?"

"No, Joe, just tired." She smiled faintly, adding: "Yoshi did say some nice things about you."

Yoshi! He felt a stab of guilt. Lord, he couldn't tell

Suzanne about his present suspicions. Through the window he saw Ebell stirring around and suppressed the thought that she would be alone that night. Bending, he kissed her lips lightly, studying her face in the growing dusk.

"Good night, sweetheart," he murmured.

"Good night, Joe." She smiled and he left, feeling that all was right with the world. Back at the house, he found Selinda waiting on the veranda.

"We've been holding supper," she explained.

"Thank you," he answered gruffly.

"Joe . . ." She reached out and touched his hand. "It's good to have you home again."

After supper Stark walked into the garden and lit a cigarette, then sat on a lawn swing to smoke and think. The wind had stiffened, becoming warm and moist, and a jumble of thunderheads, silver-rimmed from the moon, promised rain.

He had found it ironical sitting across the table from Selinda—sitting in Hawker's chair, facing Hawker's beautiful widow, the white-jacketed and impassive Obak waiting at his elbow. The span across the table was measured in scant feet, but Stark had been aware that a dead man lay between them. Not so Selinda.

Aside from the usual amenities, neither had made an attempt at conversation; but her eyes had smoldered and he had caught the taut look on her face. Hawker, he thought, is cold in his grave—cold in Selinda's heart.

A rustling came from behind him and he turned in time to see the slim form of a woman hurrying through the garden. She saw him and stopped. Yoshi! He had mistaken her for Hawker's widow. She came toward him.

"Joe . . . Joe Stark." Her voice sounded pathetically small.

"Sit down, Yoshi," he heard himself saying.

Instead, she remained standing, staring down at him, her face a blur in the darkness. Remembering Talo's accusation, he returned her look wonderingly.

107

"Do you believe what I told you last night?" she whispered.

"Yes, I believe you." He answered almost without thinking, without deliberation, knowing without knowing that it was true. She took a step forward, then sat on the edge of the swing facing him.

"You're a strange man," she said.

"Why strange?" He smiled and she didn't answer. Rubbing her hands nervously, she looked away, then laid them on her lap and brought her eyes back to meet his, saying, "I have something to tell you."

"Say it," he encouraged.

"The Japanese attack . . ." Her voice faltered.

"Go on," he said.

"It's due tomorrow."

"You know that?" he pressed.

"Yes, I know it." She spoke in a flat monotone. "The date is set—it's certain."

"The time?"

"That I don't know."

"Who told you, Yoshi?"

She fumbled with her hands and said, "I can't tell you."

He asked shrewdly, "Your father?"

This time she stared levelly at him and her hands became composed again. She said quietly, "No, not him."

"But you do know the attack is coming. That's definite?"

"It's definite," she replied.

"All right, Yoshi." He stared into the night, thinking: *The wait is over. Now we blow the works.* For some reason, he felt glad.

"Joe . . ." He turned as she spoke, seeing the wistfulness in her face, thinking it sad and beautiful at the same time. "I don't want you to think too badly of me," she added.

"Does my opinion mean so much to you?" he asked curiously.

"Yes," she answered softly.

"Yet you hated me last night," he reminded her.

"At first—not later."

108

"Because I wasn't like Hawker?" he asked.

"Yes, that was it." She brooded a moment. "You could have had me, and didn't."

"That's not the way I operate, Yoshi."

"I know that now." Abruptly she rose, turning to stare down at him. He watched her face, thinking again it was beautiful. Her words came low: "Now I wish it had been otherwise."

She fled before he could answer, vanishing in the darkness in the direction of the infirmary. A sadness came over him. Yoshi was strange, strange and beautiful, and somehow her life had been marred. The net of circumstances had been flung, had fallen over her. For a moment, he too, wished it had been otherwise. He shook the feeling aside and rose from the swing. The attack was coming. He had things to do. . . . He let them run through his mind, feeling the cool wind against his face.

Holden held the powerhouse, Texas Smith guarded the vital oil reservoirs, Jasper Hodges was downstream at the Plaju refinery; the handful of drillers stationed along the jungle pipeline and at the distant wells would complete their jobs and make their way to Sunda Strait. All that had been arranged.

The rest of them would use the river launch, but it would have to be checked, supplies moved. A job for Gurko, he thought. He found himself walking toward Ebell's house and quickened his step. The sound of movement came from inside before Suzanne answered his knock, clutching her bathrobe together at the throat.

"Let me in," he urged impatiently.

"Joe . . ."

She sounded cold and he said quickly, "There's trouble. We've got to talk."

"Oh." A catch came in her voice as she stepped aside for him to enter, then quietly closed the door. "Wait till I light the lamp," she whispered. She rustled around and the light came on, then she turned to face him.

"The attack's coming tomorrow," he said swiftly. "I don't know what time—maybe morning, maybe evening, but you've got to be ready to get out of here on a second's notice."

"I'd better tell Dad."

"I'll alert him. I'll pass the word along—tell Selinda, the Hodges . . ."

"I'll tell Yoshi," she suggested.

He stared at her, saying, "She knows."

"Oh?" She cocked her head inquisitively.

"She's the one I learned it from," he said gravely.

"Oh," she repeated, her lips forming a small oval as she drew the word out. He told her what he knew.

"So you see, I really wasn't persecuting her," he finished.

"I know that now." Looking anxiously at him, she said, "I know who you really are, Joe."

He experienced a momentary relief. "Who told you?"

"Martha. Jasper told her," she explained.

"Does it make any difference to you?" he asked.

"No, it makes me feel better. Now I know that you were just doing your job." Her eyes caught his in a beseeching look, and she added: "Be honest with me, Joe. We haven't much time, have we?"

He started to deny it, but held back the words and instead said, "I don't know—I honestly don't. We should be safe once we get on the river; Vandervoort's arranged with the Navy to have us picked up at the Sunda rendezvous. I guess it depends on how hard the Japs hit—how much time we have afterward."

Staring away, she said, "I've been a fool."

"No," he countered.

She swung back toward him. "Yes, I have. We've had such a brief time . . . one glorious night. Then, because of my pride . . ." Her tongue touched her lips before she added: "Now we're only sure of tonight."

He reassured softly: "Don't be regretful. We'll have years. I'll make it that way."

"You'll try, Joe, but you can't say for sure." She smiled wanly.

110

"No, I can't," he admitted. They stared at each other and the pensive look on her face tugged at his heart. She stood straight, clasping her gown at the throat, and the room grew very quiet. Stirring, she swayed toward him, whispering, "Kiss me."

He gathered her in his arms and touched her lips with his, moving them in a soft caress over her face, feeling her respond and drawing her still closer. The thump of her heart reminded him of the fluttering of a little bird in a cage. Moving her mouth to his ear, she murmured, "I won't be foolish any longer."

"Hush," he said, kissing her with growing passion, for a moment forgetful of everything except the girl in his arms. Her body was warm, vibrant, and he caught the delicate scent of a fragrant perfume. She pushed her face into his shoulder and a tremor ran through her body.

"I love you," he whispered.

"I love you, too." She began twisting away, then caught his hands, and urged, "We've only hours."

"Don't talk," he countered, fearful lest the magic of the moment be broken. She wiped her eyes and he saw they were wet.

"I'll have to make up for the years," she promised.

"Hush, darling, just kiss me."

She moved into his arms again and clung to him, kissing and whispering endearments, pausing only to listen to his soft words. He moved his hands slowly down her body, thinking every plane and curve a perfection. His hands could almost encircle her dainty waist. Finally she pushed herself away and for an instant her eyes held the same look he had seen in Selinda's.

"Kisses aren't enough," she whispered.

"No." She wrung the admission from him.

Stepping back and without moving her eyes from his face, she threw off her gown and let it drop at her feet. He felt a catch in his throat, thinking he'd never seen a more beautiful woman. He told her so.

"You're a vision of loveliness," he whispered. She

glanced toward her room, caught his hands and moved backward, drawing him through the doorway beyond the lamplight.

Again they kissed, fervently and hungrily. For a while they held each other on the edge of the bed, locked tightly in an embrace that made him feel as if they were forever inseparable. After a while he released her and she moved her head toward the pillow.

"Now," she whispered, drawing him down upon her, fitting his hard, lean length to her voluptuous curves and warm hollows, maneuvering toward the ultimate union that neither could any longer postpone.

And if their first coming together had been a revelation, this one was a miracle beyond his experience. For a girl so inexperienced to accept every sensual refinement which a man's desire thrusts upon her—that was startling enough. What was incredible was her own fiercely uninhibited response.

For as their bodies seemed to fuse at every point, nerve ends coming erect with exquisite sensation, hers miraculously opened . . . received . . . and closed fiercely about him, to begin the frenzied ritual dance of love. . . . Now they moved with a slowly mounting fury, that was both a soaring flight to the stars and a headlong plunge into the abyss—a pulsing voyage of endless sensation, to the end of the flesh's endurance, when it must explode in unbearable delight.

With a wild cry of joy, Suzanne fell back spent—as if, should this night indeed be their last, she had at least known a woman's ultimate fulfillment.

❀ twelve

THE HANDS of Stark's watch showed one o'clock when he went out into the night, leaving Suzanne sleeping. There were no lights showing at the Hodges and he realized Jasper might be gone several hours yet.

A single light burned in the office of the Hawker house. Turning toward it, he spotted the beams of a car's headlights on the road from the powerhouse and quickened his step. The pickup pulled up and Texas Smith leaped out.

"Trouble—the coolies have taken over the powerhouse!" he exclaimed. When Stark looked aghast, he slapped his holster and continued: "I saw some activity around there while I was patrolling the reservoir. When I went over, someone took a shot at me. It was Talo—he yelled for me to stay away or he'd kill me."

"Talo." Somehow Stark wasn't surprised. He asked quietly, "Then they've got Holden?"

"I don't think so," Smith replied. "I demanded to see Pete but they said he wasn't there. Unless they killed him," he added.

"He was armed, wasn't he?"

"Yeah, a forty-five," Smith answered.

"Was he the kind of guy to go to sleep on watch?"

"No," Smith replied bluntly. "Pete had some faults but that wasn't one of them."

Stark smiled curiously, the glimmer of a suspicion in his mind. Briefly he told the other about the impending attack, without revealing how he'd learned of it. Finishing, he said, "We've got to take the powerhouse."

"Damned tootin' we do, but it's going to be tough. That place is built like a fort—one door and a couple of high

113

windows. A few armed coolies could hold it for a week."

"Dynamite would destroy the demolition switches," Stark mused.

"We can't do that," Smith objected.

"You'd better get back," Stark counselled. "Stay under cover and keep your eyes on the place. I'll work out something."

"What about Holden?" Smith demanded.

"That's one of the things I'm going to work on." He didn't explain how nor did Smith ask. He added: "I'll alert everyone—get them ready."

"The doc's at the hospital," Smith said.

"Yeah, I know. Is he safe?" He peered at the driller.

"That's one white man who's plenty safe; the Malays think he's god."

"Anyone got any weapons around here . . . rifles?" Stark asked.

"Hawker—a Savage he used on the cats. Hodges keeps a Winchester."

"We can use them." Stark stared toward the Hodges house.

Smith shifted his gunbelt and said, "I'll get along." He climbed back into the truck, waved briefly and headed back across the field.

Stark turned soward Hodges' house. The lights were out and he knocked sharply at the door, repeating it when he heard a stir inside. A minute passed before Martha answered, holding the door ajar.

"The Japanese attack is due tomorrow," Stark said crisply. "You'd better get ready to clear out."

"Tomorrow?" Sounding startled, she opened the door wider.

"Jasper home yet?"

"No, he didn't expect to return till morning." Stark saw she wore a wrap but this time her hair wasn't done up in pin curlers; it did, however, look slightly disheveled.

Hesitating, he said, "There's been trouble at the powerhouse. Holden was supposed to be there.

"Oh." She cast a quick glance over her shoulder, then looked guiltily at him.

"This is important, Martha," he said quietly.

Her eyes fell and she said simply, "All right, you know anyway. He'll be right out. He's just getting ready."

"Thank you," he replied gravely. Suppressing the impulse to state what Holden's dereliction had caused, he said instead, "Better have him go right out. Tell him to stay clear until he contacts Smith; he's keeping an eye on the place. He'd better take Jasper's Winchester."

"I'll tell him." She lifted her head defiantly. "I'm sorry, Joe. I tried to tell you something of this the other day."

"Forget it. Everyone slips," he said gruffly.

She smiled wanly. "There was bound to be trouble sooner or later."

"There needn't be."

"I hope not," she replied fervently.

Returning to the Hawker house, he thought: So Talo had been the key after all. Could he be Saito? He pushed the idea around in his mind and finally rejected it. More likely the slim *mandur* was Saito's agent—an *agent provocateur* whose task lay in assuring the big plant would be saved. If so, he was doing his job well. Accusing Yoshi had been a clever subterfuge to conceal his own activities. He thought it sounded good except for one thing: Yoshi knew the intimate details of the assault.

He found Gurko Singh waiting on the veranda. Hesitating, Stark related the situation at the powerhouse. The giant Bengali listened, caressing the blade of his kris; but when Stark finished, his eyes remained blank.

"The thing we have to do is get Talo," Stark stated emphatically.

Singh's lips formed in the semblance of a smile. "Gurko get Talo," he said softly.

"How?" He watched the Bengali, puzzled.

"Call Talo, talk with Talo." Singh stroked the blade again and added reassuringly: "Talo talk."

"Good, you've got a job."

115

Singh raced the battered sedan across the field. The powerhouse loomed up, its windows dark, and he removed his foot from the gas pedal and began braking. When they were stopped, Stark hopped out, glancing first at the powerhouse and then at the hulking Bengali. Singh spoke first.

"When Talo come out, Gurko grab him."

"How will you get him out?" he asked curiously.

Singh looked at him without expression, saying simply, "Gurko say he got message."

"All right, we'll try it." Stark shook his shoulders impatiently. "We'd better approach from the blind side."

They plodded across the field and the squat form of the powerhouse loomed larger. Dark, it looked lifeless and abandoned; Stark knew better. Talo waited there—Talo and a crew of hand-picked Malays, no doubt. The slim Malay with the implacable eyes had been selected as Hawker's *mandur* because of his intelligence and loyalty, only the loyalty had been warped in another direction.

In the distance, lamplight filtered from the windows of the field hospital. Ebell would be there caring for the sick, unmindful of what else might be occurring. The huge plant and its oil so precious to the Japs were minor considerations; only human life counted, regardless of race, color or creed. Stark felt a quiet admiration for the man. Singh stopped and gestured. A few seconds later Smith's voice came from the darkness.

"That you, Stark?"

"I'm with Gurko." He watched the driller approach. "We're going to pull Talo out of there—get some answers," he added.

"How?"

"Gurko says he can do it."

"If Gurko says he can, he can," Smith declared. "We'll have to watch our step. I spotted someone on the roof."

Stark gazed at the building without answering. The roof would make any approach impossible were it not for the night, but even so he'd have to use care. He switched his eyes to the driller.

116

"Stay here, watch for Holden. He'll be along pretty quick."

Smith hesitated before answering, "Okay, will do."

He didn't ask about Holden and Stark suspected he had already guessed the answer. He nodded at Gurko and they started ahead, walking more slowly as they drew near the building. Reaching it, they pressed their bodies against the brick wall and moved to one corner, then slipped around it until they were within several feet of the door. Gurko leaned over and whispered, "Tuan wait."

Stark nodded, knowing the futility of questions. The Bengali left the safety of the wall and walked into the open, stopping six or eight feet from the door. Stark checked his automatic and waited.

Suddenly Gurko Singh bellowed, standing with legs astride. For an instant there was dead silence before the quick sound of startled voices came from the interior of the powerhouse. Singh called again, speaking in Malay.

The rasp of hinges shattered the night and Stark crouched, seeing a furtive shadow slip from the building— a Malay with a rifle. Pointing it at the Bengali, he spoke in a liquid tongue and Singh answered, at the same time starting slowly toward the doorway. The native, watching him, backed slowly toward Stark. Some more words were exchanged, this time between Gurko Singh and someone standing in the doorway. Instinctively Stark knew it was Talo.

Speaking rapidly, Singh had almost reached the door when the Malay with the rifle moved it up and spoke sharply. Singh bellowed, sprang forward with the quickness of a cat, shooting out his hands and almost as quickly leaping backward, this time with a slight, writhing figure in his grip. The Malay sentry swung the rifle to catch Singh in his sights and Stark shot him.

Half a dozen figures boiled from the building swinging clubs and parangs. Stark's automatic spat fire several times. He caught movement in the periphery of his eye, whirled and lashed out, smashing one of the attackers against the brick wall.

117

Catching the falling body, he used it as a shield, pushing the man ahead of him as he tried to reach the door. A blade whistled through the air, struck his victim, and Stark felt the warm splash of blood against his cheek. Gurko Singh was kicking at his assailants, trying to maintain his clutch on Talo. The *mandur* writhed like a snake, screaming commands. Two Malays circled the Bengali, watching for a chance to cut him down.

Stark hurled the body at them and fired twice, seeing the two natives stagger and fall. Whirling, he threw his shoulder against the door a split second after it slammed and a bolt shot into place. He bounced back, feeling as if he'd broken a bone, then swung to face the Bengali. Gurko stood with his legs astride, holding the Malay over his head as if he were a doll. The *mandur* had ceased his struggles, lying inert in the Bengali's huge hands.

"Talo," he grunted.

"Let's get out of here," Stark rasped, remembering the danger from the roof. Laughing, Gurko wheeled and raced across the field still holding Talo aloft. Stark followed at his heels. A rifle roared from somewhere behind them and a bullet whizzed past his head. They dropped to a crouch, weaving through the darkness until Smith's voice halted them. Stark saw a second figure and recognized the lean build of the man as that of Holden.

"Told you Gurko could do it," Texas Smith commented, when they reached his side. The Bengali plunked down the *mandur,* retaining a grasp on his arm. They watched them, blank-faced. Stark saw Singh's eyes probing the field in the direction of the powerhouse.

"Hear sumpin'?" Holden asked.

"He hears coolies," Smith said. "A couple of them have probably come outside. We make pretty good targets here." Stark stared at the Bengali, who nodded agreement. Making a decision, he turned to Smith.

"You and Holden stick around. We'll take Talo back, put him through the wringer."

"Kill the sonuvabitch," Texas Smith suggested.

118

Glancing at the *mandur,* Stark said, "We might do that. It depends on his willingness to talk." He glanced at Singh. "Take him to the car."

"Yes, Tuan."

The Bengali flung Talo up at arm's length and strode toward the sedan. Talo made no sound, no move to resist. Stark drove, feeling the wind buffet the car, aware the hours were speeding too fast.

Drawing up in front of the Hawker house, he nodded wordlessly toward the office and Gurko Singh got out, pulling the *mandur* after him. Headlights gleamed from the river road and Stark realized it must be Hodges returning.

"Take him inside," he ordered. "I'll be along in a minute."

"Yes, Tuan." The Bengali flung the *mandur* over his shoulder and strode toward the veranda. Stark turned to await the oncoming car. It pulled to a stop and Hodges leaped out.

"We gotta get ready to move," Hodges yelled. "We might get hit at dawn."

"That early?" Stark questioned sharply.

"The Dutch trapped a Jap agent." The man's face and voice were panicky and his breath stank of whiskey.

Stark told him about the trouble at the powerhouse, ending: "Talo's at the office now."

"Then we won't be able to destroy the plant?"

"We'll destroy it," Stark assured him. "I'll work on Talo."

"We haven't time," Hodges insisted. "We have to get out now."

"Not till we do what we have to do."

"Damn you, Stark, you've held things up too long," Hodges shouted. He stared at the ONI man, panting heavily, then wheeled and stomped toward his house. Stark went to the office and found Talo sitting in a corner chair, guarded by Singh.

Without preamble, he stared at the *mandur* and said, "I need information and I'm going to get it, and after I

119

get it, you're going to call your men out of the powerhouse. Gurko might have to break every bone in your body. It depends on you."

When the *mandur* returned his stare unflinchingly, Stark gestured and Singh came across the room like a cat, catching the Malay, twisting him around and pushing his wrist toward his shoulder blade. He watched the ONI man for directions. Stark eyed the *mandur* musingly. No time for niceties, for subtle attempts at persuasion—the clock was spinning too fast for that. Words alone wouldn't do the trick: Talo's eyes told him as much. Stark moved his head—Gurko inched up on the arm. Sweat broke out on the Malay's face.

"Harder," Stark commanded.

Gurko moved his arm again and Talo winced. Hearing footsteps, Stark turned as Selinda paused in the doorway. Her eyes moved from Stark to Singh, finally settling on Talo. She wore the white robe again and appeared as composed as if she were sitting at the dinner table facing a guest. Her eyes came back to Stark.

"Trouble?" she asked quietly. He told her. When he finished she spoke to Talo in Malay. Stark stared at Singh for some guide to what she was saying but the Bengali gave no sign. Talo replied and she got a startled expression.

"He says Yoshi ordered the taking of the powerhouse," she exclaimed.

"I imagine he would say that." Stark smiled faintly. "He accused Yoshi of being a Jap agent before. It seems strange that he's now carrying out her orders."

Selinda spoke to Talo again and there was a rapid-fire exchange of words.

"He says Yoshi threatened him with death from the steel needle," she told Stark, adding: "He means a blowgun."

"Is that true?" Stark demanded. Talo nodded sullenly. Stark motioned and Gurko inched the arm up again. The sweat hung from the *mandur's* face in large drops and his jaw muscles corded. Stark switched his gaze to Selinda;

120

she had her eyes riveted on the suffering man, yet her face showed no compassion.

"Is that true?" Stark asked loudly.

Talo grimaced and nodded, pulled back his head in an expression of pain and whispered, "Yes, Tuan."

"Do you know when the Jap attack is coming?" Stark thundered.

"No, Tuan."

"Pressure," he snapped.

Singh worked methodically; the *mandur* suddenly gasped, his head rolling forward. Stark lifted his chin and saw he was unconscious. He glanced at Selinda, sensing the crinkle of amusement on her lips.

"I'll have Obak get some coffee," she suggested. He stared incredulously at her, thinking she had nerves of ice. The quick patter of feet came from the veranda and Martha Hodges pushed open the door.

"Jasper's packing his things, says he's going to leave," she exclaimed. "He ordered me to get ready."

"Leave how?" Stark searched her face.

"The launch. He's going to take it."

Stark swung toward Singh. "Stay here—watch him. I'll be right back." He glanced at Martha. "Come on, we'll settle this." She nodded and followed him from the house, catching his hand at the bottom of the stairs.

"Don't hurt him, Joe."

"I won't."

She trudged at his side until they reached the porch. Hodges met them at the door and eyed his wife malevolently, demanding, "Where's my rifle?"

She looked startled but Stark said smoothly, "Holden has it. I sent him for it."

"Damn it, you had no right."

"What's this about leaving?" Stark cut in.

Hodges glared at his wife. "So, you sneaked off—told him."

"Please, Jasper."

"I've got a good mind to leave you here—let your boy friends take care of you," he snarled.

121

"Knock it off," Stark warned.

Hodges turned angrily. "You think I don't know about her slutting around?"

"I said to shut up," he said sharply. "Now what's this about leaving?"

Hodges licked his lips. "That's right, there's nothing we can do now."

"You're not leaving," Stark said quietly. "If you do, I'll get you, if I have to follow you to the ends of the earth."

"Are you threatening me?" Hodges demanded.

"Damned tootin', I am. Martha can get ready and stand by the launch with the other women; you'll be needed in the field."

"Of course, I wasn't planning—"

"Okay, we've got it straight," Stark interrupted. He glanced at Martha, saw the tiredness and strain in her face before she turned back into the house.

He hurried first to Yoshi's cottage, rapping lightly on the door. The creak of bedsprings followed by the movement of her feet across the floor reached him.

"Who's there?"

"Stark," he answered.

She rustled around and lit the lamp, then opened the door, saying softly, "I was asleep. Won't you come in?"

"There's no time," he told her. Nevertheless he stepped inside and paused, looking down at her, thinking the flowered kimono and bunched hair gave her the appearance of a fragile doll. "We're getting the evacuation party ready. You'd better prepare, go down to the launch," he ended.

"Yes, of course." She stared fixedly at him.

"I'll see you there," he promised. She took a step toward him and halted.

"Good-by, Joe Stark," she whispered.

"Not good-by. It'll only be for a while."

"Yes—just for a while." Her face looked waxen under the lamplight.

Going outside he saw the first glimmer of dawn in the

east, a gray light against a leaden sky, and he wondered where the night had fled. The wind, cool and heavy with moisture, carried a promise of rain.

Entering Ebell's house, he found Suzanne still sleeping. She had pulled a sheet over her body and lay with her head in the crook of her arm. He lit the lamp and sat on the edge of the bed, bent forward and softly kissed her cheek. She stirred, opening her eyes.

"It's time to go, honey," he said.

✿ thirteen

SEVERAL HOURS passed before Stark finally got on the road to the powerhouse. They had checked the river launch, laid in an extra supply of fuel, clothing and provisions, and had rehearsed their escape tactics. Suzanne had remained at the launch while the other women gathered their last few belongings.

Stark drove slowly under a gray, troubled sky, avoiding the ruts. Sullen and bleary-eyed, Hodges huddled against the opposite door, his face covered with a gray stubble of beard, his breath with the sour smell of whiskey. Talo, glum and withdrawn, sat in the rear seat alongside Gurko Singh, his eyes fixed straight ahead. Whatever drama would unfold this day would come under stormy skies, Stark thought. The wind had picked up, raw and gusty, blowing in from the strait in the manner of a gathering *sumatra* and the tumbled cloud masses spoke of torrential rains.

Approaching the cracking plant he saw neither smoke nor steam, and realized the furnaces had been damped— the huge plant had died and now awaited only the formal ceremony of destruction.

He stared ahead, momentarily glad that Hawker

123

couldn't see it. With the pumps stopped, fires banked and all work stilled, he found something solemn in the scene, like gazing at the ruins of an ancient city whose people were dust, he thought. Ahead, Texas Smith appeared at the side of the road and waved, followed by the lean, saturnine Holden. Drawing up alongside them, he saw their clothes were smeared with mud and oil, and the taller driller held Hodges' rifle. Smith rested his hand on his holster.

"We're opening the valves, letting the oil flow into the fire walls," he explained.

Hodges sat up straight. "Who gave that order?"

"I did," he snapped.

"He's right—it's time," Stark cut in.

"There's a couple of men on the powerhouse roof," Smith warned. "I saw 'em poking their heads over."

"Great," Stark commented.

"You'll have to make a dash for it." He shifted his eyes to Hodges. "How about taking over for me—help Pete open the valves? I'll give a hand ahead."

"I'll be glad to," Hodges promptly replied.

When he had changed places with the Texan, Stark looked at him and warned: "You'd better check the lines again."

"Sure, don't worry. Pete and I'll take care of everything," Hodges responded. Holden nodded affirmatively, his eyes somber. Stark threw the car into gear, picking up speed on the muddy road.

Texas Smith held his head cocked, staring through the windshield, and after a while said, "Yep, a couple of people topside."

Stark didn't reply, thinking he'd have to alert Ebell at the field hospital. After a minute he raised his voice: "Here we go. Keep your heads down."

He tromped on the accelerator and as the car leaped ahead, began swerving from side to side on the road to make as difficult a target as possible. The powerhouse sped toward them. The car struck a series of ruts and bounced, swaying, several times coming perilously close

124

to the edge of the road before he regained control. He had the impression of a buffeting wind.

"Someone sighting in," Smith yelled.

"Keep your heads down!"

"Hell, those gooks can't shoot—" He chopped off the words as a hole appeared in the windshield just above their line of vision. Glass spattered against Stark's face and he instinctively ducked, yanking the wheel and swerving to the side of the road. As the wheels spun wildly in the mud, he shifted down, letting up on the throttle before they caught hold again. He picked up speed, too busy watching the road to worry about the roof. All at once the powerhouse wall filled the windshield. At the last instant he swerved, skidded to a halt and leaped out.

A Malay popped his head over the edge of the roof, screamed something and brought a rifle into view. Stark crouched and fumbled for his automatic, hearing a sharp crack before he could get it out. The Malay's body straightened in a stiff, agonized movement, swayed forward and toppled over the edge, turning in the air like a slow pinwheel before thudding against the ground.

Smoke drifted above the barrel of Smith's .45. He held the weapon loosely, almost negligently, slightly above the level of the holster. His eyes held an intent gleam. Lord, they had to get inside, Stark thought, and yelled, "Get Talo!"

Gurko Singh popped to his side, one huge hand clasping his hapless victim's shoulder. "Order them to open the door," Stark rasped.

Talo hesitated and Singh's grip tightened.

"Tell 'em," Stark snarled.

The *mandur* bit his lip, then called out in the liquid language of his people. Stark glanced at the Bengali, satisfied when the latter nodded affirmatively. After a brief silence, the sound of movement came from the inside; Talo called again. Stark tensed, waiting, feeling the seconds build into a long silence before the click of a bolt reached him.

Grabbing the *mandur* as a shield, he kicked open the

125

door and leaped in. A waiting Malay sprang forward wielding a parang, but hurling Talo to one side Stark whipped up the automatic and fired. The man spun, his knees buckled, and the blade clattered to the floor. Half a dozen screaming natives rushed him.

Smith's heavy weapon boomed twice alongside his shoulder and the acrid smell of cordite stung his nostrils. Glimpsing a figure rushing in from the side, he whirled, smashed the barrel of his automatic into a slender brown face and followed through with a brutal judo smash against the base of the man's neck.

Bellowing, Gurko Singh pushed his way past Smith and plunged into the melee with his kris whirling. The Malays broke ranks and abruptly the fight ended. Three or four bodies cluttered the floor, while the survivors crouched against the opposite wall, their eyes terrified. At Stark's command, Gurko Singh gathered up their weapons.

Smith, reloading his forty-five, asked suddenly, "Where's Talo?"

Stark swung around, a glance sufficing to tell him that in the confusion the *mandur* had made his escape.

"To hell with him," Smith added. "We've got a job to do." He indicated the demolition equipment, now a shambles of torn wiring. Inspecting it briefly, he added, "It can be repaired—a helluva job."

"We'd better get at it," Stark decided. Smith nodded and hitched up his gunbelt. They worked quickly and silently, untangling the broken wiring and splicing the ends together while Gurko Singh guarded the captives. Stark worried a bit about Ebell and finally mentioned it to Smith.

"You'd better check him," the Texan drawled. "The doc probably doesn't know there's a war going on."

"That's what I'm thinking." He straightened up, glanced around the powerhouse, then went outside and headed toward the field hospital.

Ebell was holding a stethoscope to a patient's chest when he entered. Standing inside the door, he surveyed the room. Four patients—Ebell had it whipped he thought, feeling a quick relief. None of them looked too sick. The doctor raised his head inquiringly.

"Time to go," Stark announced cheerfully. "Suzanne —the others—are at the evacuation station. We expect an attack at any time."

Ebell didn't answer immediately, but let his eyes roam along the row of empty cots and at the four remaining patients before saying, "I'm staying here as long as anyone remains that needs my help."

"The others need your help, too," he replied crisply.

"They're not sick," Ebell rebuked.

Stark studied his face, noting the deep lines of fatigue and the tiredness in his eyes. He said, "These men are almost well."

"I'm remaining," Ebell broke in curtly.

"There's not much use of that. When this place goes, it'll go like a torch, and when the Japanese move in . . ." He didn't finish, contemplating the other speculatively.

"I'm a physician, Stark." The remark told him that argument was useless.

"All right," he said finally. "We'll be colse by . . . at the powerhouse."

"And I'll be here." Ebell stared at his patient, fingering his stethoscope, while Stark regarded him with mixed feelings, thinking his attitude was commendable—and foolhardy. There was nothing he could do once the Japanese came—nothing except die. He went outside and hurried toward the powerhouse. The whipping wind and massive storm clouds were a welcome sight; maybe the *sumatra* would break, hold back the attack. . . .

Holden had returned during his absence to report more damage to the lines. Tersely Smith told him about it— repairs were being rushed. When he finished, they debated what to do with their captives. Gurko Singh listened, fingering his kris significantly. His face took on visible disappointment at the decision to free them and chase them from the compound. At Stark's order, he herded them outside where they broke and fled toward the distant

127

rim of the jungle, their speed telling of their haste to be free of the Bengali's grim eye. Smith looked up as Stark returned inside.

"The machine shop's not mined," he commented. "Hawker was going to have the Malays destroy it with sledges."

"We'll get it." Stark glanced at his watch, surprised to find it past noon.

He motioned the Bengali outside, then got the pickup truck and drove to the reservoir area. They helped Holden and Hodges with the lines until Stark realized the situation was under control, then left for the machine shop. As they drove past the silent cracking plant the wind slackened and the mist seemed to become less gray—like passing through the eye of a storm, he thought. Although clouds blanketed the sun, the day grew sultry. The machine shop drew nearer and driving alongside it, he parked. Inside they found sledge hammers and turned toward the stilled machines.

Stark worked with a fury, sweating, feeling the tension drain from his body as he moved methodically down the rows of expensive machinery, the smash of the sledge against the metal stinging his hands.

He paused several times to catch his breath and watch his giant companion. Gurko Singh moved with rhythmic ease, the muscles of his corded nut-brown body rippling as he swung the sledge. Saws, lathes, grinders, delicate instrument consoles—within an hour all had been reduced to rubble.

Dripping sweat and chilled at the sudden contact with the cool air, they returned to the car and started back. A mist overhung the earth and the air held still as they sped into a gray pall, a condition known to the Malays as "a silent storm."

Reaching the powerhouse, Gurko Singh got out of the car and immediately cocked his head in a listening attitude, an action that brought Stark's head up alertly. For a few seconds he heard nothing. He was looking inquiringly at the Bengali when the distant crack of gunfire broke the air. *Whap! Whap! Whap!*

Ack-ack! He studied the sky in the direction of the Plaju refineries, vexed by the veil of mist and cloud. The ack-ack spelled aircraft. He felt an odd expectancy, realizing Vandervoort couldn't long delay his decision.

Scanning the field, he caught sight of Hodges at the far side of the reservoirs, a small figure moving between the great earthen wall embankments. *Wa-hoooom!* A low series of rumbles rolled out of the west, overwhelming the lower voices of the guns. Turning, he ran into the powerhouse.

"They've just blown the Plaju plants. How soon before we're ready to go?"

"Not long," Smith answered imperturbably.

"We'll have to hurry."

Smith said laconically, "We are hurrying. I've almost got it."

Stark saw there was nothing he could do and went outside. The sharp crack of ack-ack came between deeper booming explosions and he fancied he felt the ground tremble under him. He stared at his watch, startled to find the afternoon far gone. A growing roar came from the sky and it took his several seconds to identify it as that of airplane engines.

Two float Zeros emerged from the mist, made a low pass over the oil reservoirs and vanished. He scanned the field, hoping Hodges and Holden had finished their jobs; a sense of fleeing time plagued him. The huge oil tanks appeared like giant behemoths hiding in the mist, and he thought: *A hell of a day for an attack.*

Texas Smith came out. Bare-headed and wet with sweat, his shirt clung to his thin body and the .45 appeared ludicrous against his thin hips. Cupping his hands, he yelled, "I'll start the generators."

Stark felt a surge of relief. After a while he heard the cough of a gasoline engine, breaking into a steady chug-chug; the sound of the generator that supplied booster current to the demotion switches was reassuring.

129

Texas Smith came back around the corner wiping his face and asked, "Any sign of Pete or Hodges?"

"I saw Hodges once . . . at the far side."

"They ought to be along," he observed. Briefly studying the field, he turned back into the powerhouse. Stark started to follow when he spotted a car speeding across the field and halted, held by an uneasy presentiment. Suzanne! He knew it even before she skidded the car to a stop and leaped out, running toward him. He caught her, holding her and feeling her quick breath before she raised her face and spoke.

"Dad didn't come, then I heard shooting and got scared."

"He's still at the field hospital," he explained, stroking her hair. "It's dangerous here. You shouldn't have come."

"I couldn't wait. There was just Martha and me."

"How about Selinda and Yoshi?" he asked sharply.

"I don't know. They were supposed to come later but they never showed up. That's one of the things that worried me. I'd better get Dad," she finished.

"I'll send Gurko," he said swiftly. He shot an order to the Bengali before she could protest. He was staring after Singh when her voice penetrated his consciousness again.

"It's time, isn't it, Joe?"

"Yes, it's time." He turned to look toward the oil tanks, wishing Hodges and Holden would hurry.

She pushed the side of her face against his shoulder and murmured, "I'm glad for what we've had."

"It's not ended," he replied, trying to put conviction into the words. "Postponed perhaps—not ended." The sound of airplanes came again and he jerked up his head. The sky seemed to part, a float Zero thundered past and behind it a brilliant orange light exploded above the reservoirs.

Parachute flare! It dropped, swaying, its flame-colored light reflected eerily against the low cloud banks, and he knew the light in daytime was intended to mark a point. For what? He felt Suzanne tremble and laid his hand reassuringly on her arm. Another thunder shook the air as two huge flying boats came through the mists spilling small bundles from their bellies. The bundles jerked, slowing abruptly in mid-air, exploding into white hemispheres. Christ—paratroops!

He swung toward Suzanne and rasped, "Get in the car—back to the landing!"

"Not without you and Dad."

"Do what I tell you," he exclaimed harshly. He pushed her toward the car and shouted for Smith. The Texan popped from the powerhouse.

"Paratroops," Stark snapped. "Stand by to blow the works."

"What about Pete and Hodges?"

"We can't wait." He scanned the sky. The swinging chutes were riding down.

"Joe?" He whirled, saw the stricken look on Suzanne's face and forced his voice to hardness.

"Get in the car—quick!"

"I'll be waiting."

She fled before he could answer and he swung his attention back to the field. The paratroopers were landing, fighting the shroud lines as they tried to keep the chutes from dragging them over the field. A slim figure dashed toward the Japanese waving a flag of the Rising Sun. Talo! A rifle shot split the air and one of the paratroopers staggered, falling forward on his face. A few seconds later a figure emerged from between the fire wall enclosures running in a low crouch.

"Pete," Smith barked. Holden halted abruptly and brought the rifle to his shoulder. *Crack!* Talo, waving the Japanese flag and gesticulating toward the powerhouse, took a single step forward and sank to the ground. Holden raced forward, panting heavily as he reached their side.

"Christ, a million Japs," he exclaimed.

"Where's Hodges?" Stark demanded.

"He saw them—ducked."

"We can't wait." Texas Smith's face got hard. Stark nodded and he vanished into the powerhouse. Hearing a shout, Stark turned, seeing Gurko Singh and the doctor.

131

The latter reached his side, gasping for breath as he exclaimed, "Where's Suzanne?"

"In the car. Get her out of here," Stark ordered.

"How about you?" ﹨

"We'll follow in the pickup."

Ebell's face grew apologetic. "My patients got scared and ran away," he explained.

"Good," Stark snapped without humor. "You'd better hurry." He flashed a glance at the girl and saw the terror in her face.

"Get going, we'll follow," he shouted. She moved her head in a small jerk of acknowledgment as her father ran toward her. The float Zeros came around again and Stark switched his attention to the sky. Another flying boat came through the mist dropping its human cargo.

Whoo-hooom! A low rumble rolled across the field, the ground shook and livid tongues of flame speared the sky, reaching up and gathering in the floating hemispheres of billowing silk. Stark watched, fascinated at the frantic gyrations of the small specks at the ends of the shroud lines as they disappeared into the sea of flame. The fire bases flattened and expanded and, triggered by a series of explosions, mushroomed out into the wide lanes between the reservoirs, for a moment obliterating the landscape. Subsiding, they settled into a score of vast fire rings, each spearing angrily at the sky.

Small figures became visible between the walls of flame, and a wave of heat struck Stark's body. With it came the acrid scent of burning oil. The cracking plant shuddered and collapsed with a deep-throated roar, its skeletal girders twisted at crazy angles. Beyond it the foundry lay in a ragged heap. Several thin, high screams pierced the air and two flaming figures dashed into view, human torches that finally fell and lay still, like fireballs come to rest.

"Jasper!" Holden exclaimed. Stark saw the superintendent at the same instant. He was scurrying between the fire lanes, his body crouched. The crackle of gunfire came and he stumbled, falling, then struggled to his knees

132

and tried to rise. Holden cursed and gripped his rifle, his face tortured.

"Goddamnit, I'll have to get him," he rasped. "I owe him that much." He dashed forward before Stark could reply. A paratrooper dashed toward Hodges and Holden shot him with scarcely a break in his stride. Stark threw a quick glance backward, dismayed to discover Suzanne and her father waiting in the car.

"Gurko's got the pickup," Smith shouted. "Get in and I'll help Pete."

"Tell Suzanne to get going and stand by with Gurko," Stark snapped.

He flipped out his automatic without waiting for an answer and started after Holden, knowing the futility of the act. Well, he had destroyed the field, done his job—now he was on his own. He saw the driller reach Hodges' side as the sharp bark of an automatic weapon split the air. Holden jerked erect, half-spun and toppled next to the superintendent.

"Back," Smith yelled. Stark cursed and stopped as several paratroopers burst into view. They paused to fire a few rounds into the fallen men before coming on again. Smith's .45 roared, Japanese rifles took up the refrain and bullets whizzed past Stark's head. Whirling, he saw Suzanne waiting with the car door open and ran toward her as Texas Smith piled into the pickup alongside Gurko Singh. Stark slid in beside her, threw the car into gear and crowded the accelerator, aware of the pickup following close behind. The chatter of gunfire followed them, gradually dying in the distance.

✿ fourteen

STARK RACED the sedan into a multicolored mist which caught and reflected the dancing flames from the furiously burning oil reservoirs. Heavy black smoke billowed skyward and the acrid smell of burning oil stung his nostrils. Remembering the flames licking at the silk chutes, he shuddered. Death came in many forms—that form he didn't relish.

The wind picked up, buffeting the car, and mud spattered against the undersides of the fenders in a steady drumming roar. The mist seemed a fluid thing, filled with movement, and he kept his eyes glued to the road, every nerve tensed for action. The pickup followed, riding close behind his bumper. Off to one side a float Zero thundered past; behind it through the gray veil of sky came a big plane spewing paratroops.

"Japanese," Ebell said tensely.

Stark felt Suzanne stiffen and pushed harder on the accelerator while he watched the billowing chutes. They came down fast, slanting with the wind, their human cargoes landing hard and fighting to gather in the shroud lines. Stark saw they'd just be able to squeeze past them.

How many paratroops had landed? He pushed the question to the back of his mind and concentrated on immediate problems. He'd have to get Yoshi and wind up some unfinished business—establish contact with Vandervoort and get the evacuation started. The Japs would move in fast. He became conscious of Suzanne again.

"We'll be clear of the paratroops in a minute," he encouraged, sensing her fear.

"I'm afraid." She huddled closer and he laid a hand over hers, feeling the coldness of her flesh, saying, "Don't

134

worry, we'll be moving upstream before you know it. Once we hit the river, we're safe."

"Safe." She echoed the word forlornly.

"Troops ahead," Ebell said edgily.

Stark snapped his attention back and saw a number of distant figures fanning across the field toward the road. He pushed the accelerator the remaining distance to the floorboard and felt the sedan gather speed. Between bouncing and swaying, it seemed to glide out of control and he got the uneasy impression of participating in a foot race on ice.

The road turned at an angle that took them away from the Japanese; he had begun to breathe easier when a gigantic fist of wind slammed the car and caused it to yaw wildly before he managed to get it under control. With the wind came rain, a deluge that sounded like the roll of drums as it beat against the metal and windshield, for a moment immobilizing the wiper blades.

"Sumatra!" Ebell yelled.

Stark nodded, grateful for the storm, hoping it would enable them to sneak past the Japanese; hoping, too, he wouldn't run off the road, for the field rapidly was taking on the appearance of a vast lake.

The wind rose in violence, hurling the rain in almost solid sheets and forcing him to slow down. The world closed around them so that nothing remained but a few feet of road—that and the car speeding through the center of a gray globe. The pickup became lost to view.

Once he glanced a Ebell. The physician's lips were compressed into a tight line and he stared straight ahead. His own nerves were icy, tense with anticipation. The world ahead blinked on and off between swipes of the wiper blades, reminding him of a blinking neon seen through a heavy fog.

A file of figures loomed out of the rain and he heard Suzanne's gasp. He caught the flickering impression of backs bent into the storm, trudging figures with slung rifles, before he cursed and moved the wheel, feeling a series of crashes as the sedan sideswiped the men at the

135

rear of the column. The car lurched and began to skid, going into a half-turn as he fought for control.

"Heads down," he snapped tersely.

Several of the Japanese were hurriedly trying to bring their rifles to bear when the pickup truck sped out of the rain and bowled them over.

Smith leaned out of the cab, firing point-blank at them. The sedan came to the end of the skid and Stark threw it into first, feeling the wheels spin in the mud for several seconds before they caught hold. He straightened the car out and began picking up speed, conscious that Gurko Singh had slowed down. For half a minute the sedan and pickup raced side by side until, finally, Stark moved into the lead. He glanced back: a wall of water had cut off the Japanese. Suzanne sat with her hands clasped over her eyes.

"It's okay, it's past," he reassured her, glancing at her father.

Ebell's face was set in anguished lines, and Stark thought how alien this must be to him. Ebell's mission of mercy rapidly was culminating in an orgy of death. After a while the rain slackened, a few familiar buildings flashed by and he realized they were near the compound headquarters. He passed the Hawker house and stopped near the infirmary. The pickup pulled up behind them as Stark slipped out from behind the wheel.

Aware of Suzanne's scrutiny, he spoke to the Bengali, indicating the sedan. "Drive them to the launch as fast as possible. If there's any trouble, shove off—don't wait for Vandervoort."

"What about you?" Suzanne blurted.

"I'll check on Yoshi and Selinda," he answered. "Don't worry. Smith and I will be right behind you in the pickup."

"Joe Stark, I didn't wait back there for you to get shot now," she exclaimed.

"I'll be all right."

"I'll go with you," Ebell cut in. "Yoshi should have been at the landing hours ago."

"No you don't, Doc. That's my job," Texas Smith stated. "You get your gal to the boat."

"We'll be right behind you," Stark repeated. Aware of the protest gathering in Suzanne's face, he swung toward the Bengali, saying sharply, "Get going, Gurko."

Singh nodded and slipped into the seat beside her.

"Joe!" She leaned forward, an anguished look on her face, then the wheels spun in the mud, caught hold, and within seconds the car vanished behind a sheet of rain.

Stark glanced toward the Hawker house, then back at the Texan. "You'd better stick with the truck—keep a sharp watch," he advised. Shivering, Smith nodded and turned toward the pickup.

Shielding his eyes against the rain, Stark broke into a run toward the infirmary. Finding it empty, he went to Yoshi's cottage and banged on the door.

"It's Stark," he shouted, wiping the water from his face. Yoshi opened the door.

"Come in," she exclaimed, stepping aside. "You're soaked. I'll get you some coffee."

"No time," he answered grimly. Stepping inside, he added: "Hell's breaking loose."

"I know, I heard the firing." She watched him with something in her eyes he couldn't quite decipher. They stared at each other silently. She wore the white comb in her hair, a flowered kimono, and her tiny feet were encased in reed slippers—scarcely the attire of someone planning on going upstream, he thought.

He became aware of the closed room, the drumming rain, of her femininity, and said, "Hurry, we have to get to the landing."

She stirred slightly. "I'm not going."

"Don't be foolish," he said harshly. "This war's started. Get your things."

"No, my place is here. I'm a nurse and I'll be needed, regardless of what happens."

"Look, Yoshi, I just went through this routine with Doc Ebell," he began.

137

"He's all right?" she interrupted.

"Yes, he's on his way to the landing—right where you're going." He searched her face. "You don't want to go because of what you told me—because of what you know about the attack."

She cast her eyes down before looking at him again.

"It's no use, Joe."

"What's no use?" he challenged.

"Everything." She uttered the word with a note of resignation.

"It's over, Yoshi," he said gently. "Now you can tell me."

"There nothing to tell." She stared at him and he saw the pain in her face. "I'm not lying. I'm not a Japanese agent."

"I know that." When she didn't reply, he added: "But your father is."

For a few seconds a silence lay between them, and finally she said, "Of course, only I didn't know. You've got to believe that. I thought he was hiding because of his nationality. I didn't know until . . . until later."

"Until he warned you to get out," he supplied.

"Yes, and then I told you immediately."

"Is he Saito?" he asked curiously.

"There is no Saito. I asked him that. It's merely a code name—to identify an operation." She bit her lip and added defiantly: "Sort of a password for a net of agents."

"Including the one here," he said without humor.

"Yes."

"Now you'd better get ready," he urged.

"No, I'm staying." She struggled visibly with her emotions before adding: "It's better this way."

"Why, Yoshi?"

"Do I need a reason, Joe?" Her eyes told him that no amount of argument would change her mind. Besides, come what may, she would be safe—perhaps safer here than on the river. The drumming rain abruptly stopped and with it the wind died, leaving a strange calm in which the silence seemed almost unnatural. Finally the chatter of distant guns came. Vandervoort would be coming upstream, he thought.

Yoshi spoke again. "That night in Telukta . . ."

"I know, your father's men," he said. "I guessed that."

She smiled wanly, seemed to gather her courage, and added: "My father suggested a source of help . . . if things got bad."

Sensing her effort to continue, he said, "I already know the name of your father's agent." Relief flooded her face and he continued: "I knew it when Gurko used the name to get Talo to open the powerhouse door. When Talo implicated you, I knew you were innocent. But I think I really knew before that." He stopped speaking, watching her, feeling the passage of time and knowing he had to go, yet strangely reluctant to do so.

Finally he forced the words: "Good-by, Yoshi." The words brought a strange sadness and regret, as if he were about to leave some part of himself behind.

"Good-by, Joe Stark." She moved forward into his arms and her warm lips brushed his cheek. He held her, feeling the softness of her body, sensing a tenderness devoid of want. She kissed his lips quickly, then broke away and fled into the next room, closing the door behind her. He stared after her, his lips forming the words: *Good-by, Yoshi.*

He went outside, feeling the stillness which had come with the break in the storm. Water dripped from the trees; in the west, between the shifting masses of gray cloud, the slanting shafts of the evening sun came like golden searchlights. The deluge had washed the air clean of the heavy smoke. Spasmodic gunfire came from the west. He slogged through the mud toward the Hawker house, waving to Smith as he passed the pickup.

He found Selinda waiting.

She was standing in the middle of the main room, almost, he thought, as if she had timed his coming. He found no surprise in her eyes. She touched her lip quickly with her tongue, but otherwise her face held the impassive

139

quality of her people. They gravely regarded each other before he spoke.

"You've lost, Selinda."

"My people have lost," she corrected in a toneless voice.

"Your people? You are an agent of the Japanese," he accused. She tossed her head defiantly, showing the first sign of emotion.

"Wrong, Joe. An agent for my people, yes. Hideki Kusaka—Yoshi's father—is merely a pawn. We were using him like he thought he was using us." A faint smile touched her lips. "There will be a nation here someday—not for the Japanese or for the Dutch, but for my people. They would have needed the oil fields."

Ebell's words exactly, he thought, but there was more to it than that. He told her so.

"It won't wash, Selinda. You've served the Japanese —killed Driscoll, Tombuk, your own husband."

"Mike—I hated him." Her voice rose questioningly. "Would I have come to your room otherwise, Joe?"

"Oh? It seems to me that I recall a slight episode involving a tiger."

"Yes, but that was before . . ." She pursed her lips, weighing him.

"Before you became my lover?" he asked brutally.

"Yes." Her eyes beseeched him. "I wouldn't have afterward, Joe. I'm a woman first."

"For Driscoll, too," he added callously. She didn't change expression.

"What's fair in war, Joe Stark?"

"Everything," he admitted. "That's why you could watch your boy, Talo, suffer," he stated ungrinningly.

"It was for his people."

"Sure. Who tipped you to Driscoll?"

"One of the natives. He heard him talking with Mike."

"Obak—your killer boy?" he challenged. Before she could answer, the sound of firing came again, very near this time. He started to speak when he saw her staring past his shoulder with fearful fascination.

"Joe!" He whirled as she shrieked, pulling himself

to one side and feeling something hot graze his neck—
striking out even before he realized his attacker was Obak.

The Malay recoiled, hefted a knife and sprang at him
again. Stark moved swiftly, caught the upraised arm and
with a fast spin of his body, flung the houseboy halfway
across the room. Obak bounded up like a cat, and for
several seconds they stared at each other.

The Malay moved first but Stark was quicker. He
avoided the flickering knife blade and sent Obak stagger-
ing backward into the kitchen with a smashing right. The
Malay crashed into an oil stove and sent it toppling to
the floor. He shook his head, snarled and came back, this
time holding the knife in a gutting position. An artist,
Stark thought. He caught the glare of flames and realized
the kitchen was afire.

Moving in a tight half-circle, he feinted with his hand
and suddenly kicked out. Obak moved to avoid the blow
and Stark brought a crushing judo chop to the side of his
neck, dropping him like a felled ox. Breathing heavily, he
stared down. Obak's head jutted from his body at an odd
angle.

Selinda uttered a short scream and fled toward her
room. He started to call after her when he heard footsteps on the veranda and whirled, reaching for his automatic as Vandervoort burst through the doorway gripping
a revolver. He looked startled at sight of Stark. He slowly
swung his eyes to Obak's body, and then the flaming
kitchen before looking back again.

"Where is Mrs. Hawker?" he demanded harshly.

His appearance brought a faint smile to Stark's lips.
Fat, dripping wet, and with his white suit smeared with
mud and oil, he presented a somewhat pathetic figure, but
Stark found nothing pathetic about the revolver gripped
in his hand.

He inclined his head, saying, "In her room."

"She's a spy; I'm placing her under arrest. We caught
two of them—broke the ring. One of them named her."
The words spilled from the Dutchman's lips while his

141

eyes came to rest on the dead Malay. "Who killed him?" he ended abruptly.

"I did," Stark answered complacently. The crackle of flames became louder and smoke rolled from the kitchen. Gunfire sounded, closer this time, and Stark added: "We'd better get the hell out of here."

Vandervoort drew himself to full height. "Not without Mrs. Hawker. I don't know when or how but she's going to answer for her treason to a court of law."

"Isn't it a little late for that?"

"It's never too late for justice," Vandervoort intoned.

He started to add something when an automatic weapon crackled, followed by the unmistakable bark of the Texan's .45. Steps pounded on the porch and a Malay policeman carrying a rifle burst into the room, speaking excitedly to the Dutchman. Vandervoort interrupted with an angry command in Malay. The policeman turned and ran from the room and he swung toward Stark, saying, "She's trying to escape. She ran out the back way."

"We'd better start trying ourselves," he suggested.

"Not till I know about Selinda Hawker," Vandervoort insisted.

"Christ, this is no time to act as judge and jury."

"Executioner, too," the Dutchman said coldly.

"What's that?"

"If my man can't catch her, he's to shoot her." Vandervoort's eyes blazed. "She's a traitor."

Stark stared at him for a second, then whirling, ran from the house. Two Japanese soldiers came into view around a corner of the Hodges house, intent on the pickup. One raised an arm and lobbed something through the air. It landed, rolled beneath the pickup and exploded with a shattering roar. At that instant Texas Smith stepped out from behind another corner of the house and his .45 barked twice. The two Japanese jerked and spun, falling heavily to the ground.

"Head for the landing," Stark yelled. "I'll meet you there."

Texas Smith waved and dashed forward to snatch an

142

automatic weapon from the body of one of the Japanese before beginning a slow backward retreat. In the failing light Stark caught a glimpse of the native policeman and started in pursuit, aware of Vandervoort puffing at his heels. The Malay crossed the border of the compound and turned into a series of small clearings that threaded beadlike through the jungle thickets.

Once Stark yelled but the slim figure only increased his gait, winding along a path through the waist-high lalang grass. Far ahead in the gathering dusk he imagined he saw Selinda Hawker's fleeting figure. In the evening light the clouds took on a rosy hue and he glanced back. The Hawker house was a mass of flame. The crackle of gunfire from the compound grew more distant and Stark suddenly realized they were in the tiger field. Swearing, he ran faster, then abruptly slowed down as he saw the still figure of the policeman on the trail ahead. The Malay turned at his approach.

"What is it?" Stark grated.

"Missee hide in lalang grass." The policeman swept his arm to indicate the large field. He was about to answer when Vandervoort drew up, puffing, fighting to catch his breath before he managed to ask, "Where is she?"

The Malay indicated the field again.

"Then find her—root her out," Vandervoort commanded.

"'No, Tuan." The policeman took a backward step, staring at the Dutchman, and even in the dusk Stark saw the fear on his face.

"No?" Vandervoort exploded. The single word bore both wrath and surprise.

"Tiger, Tuan." The Malay retreated a step.

Tiger! The hair at the back of Stark's neck bristled and he inhaled, catching a musky, pungent odor that brought a vivid flash of memory. Selinda—hiding in the lalang grass! He recalled the stalked pig and cursed, fingering his automatic.

"Tiger!" Vandervoort snorted the word, then pushed

143

his face next to the Malay's and roared, "I won't let her escape. Find her!"

"No, Tuan." The policeman's face showed his terror but he held his ground. Vandervoort glared angrily at him. Muttering in a guttural tongue, he glanced across the field and took a dozen steps forward before halting to shout:

"Selinda—Selinda Hawker! There's a tiger in the field. You'd better come out."

He walked a little farther, staring through the dusk, stopping again to repeat the warning. The silence grew immense. Stark let his eyes travel slowly across the tops of the grass while he watched for movement, conscious the carrion smell came stronger. The stillness was broken by a shrill scream of terror that rose from the far edge of the field; abruptly it broke off and the silence rushed back.

"The tiger, Tuan," the Malay gasped. For an instant Stark thought his eyes had played him a trick. Vandervoort stood immobile in the gathering darkness, studying the sweep of grass. Stark felt a strange, terrible coldness grip the pit of his stomach; slowly he became conscious of the crash of gunfire.

Abruptly Vandervoort came back, saying, "Justice has been done." His voice and demeanor changed and he anxiously added: "We'd better go. We can cross the field —intersect the road."

He glanced backward, then plunged into the lalang grass and Stark followed. When they reached the road, the Dutchman turned toward the river. Walking after him, Stark rehearsed the final scene, his mind troubled. An instant after the terror-stricken scream he fancied he had seen a shadow darting into the jungle. Imagination? He'd never know. But after all, Selinda Hawker had been a consummate actress. He pushed the thought from his mind, dwelling on Suzanne as he increased his gait.

After a while the black thread of the river drew nearer.

The End

144

INVITATION TO PASSION

"All I know is that I need you," Selinda insisted. "A woman grows old in Malaya, old before her time, and has nothing—no life, no love."

Her breasts pressed against him provocatively, her body alive with a thousand movements, her words promising infinite variations of love and passion.

For a moment, Joe Stark almost surrendered, then he pushed her away. "I'm a guest in your husband's house," he reminded her.

"Kiss me, kiss me," she demanded, surging against him hotly, determined to still his conscience and to fulfill the promises she'd just made . . .

AUTHOR'S PROFILE

Christopher Gale is the pseudonym of Jeff Sutton, a well-known writer and novelist. He was born in Los Angeles and took his master's degree in psychology at the University of California in Los Angeles.

During World War II he was a sergeant in the U. S. Marine Corps and saw action at Guadalcanal, Tarawa and Okinawa. After the war he was, by turns, a newspaper reporter and photographer, a research engineer and a public relations consultant.

He now lives in Los Angeles with his wife and two children, and his hardcover book entitled A NEW BIRD CRIES was recently published by G. P. Putnam's Sons.